THE FAMILY FROM ONE END STREET

EVE CYNTHIA RUTH GARNETT (1900–1991) arrived in London in the 1920s to study art, first at the Chelsea Polytechnic School of Art, and then at the Royal Academy Schools, where she won the Creswick Prize and a Silver Medal for landscape painting. As an artist, landscapes and murals were always her favourite forms; and there is a huge mural painted by her at the Children's House in Bow, London.

In 1927, she was commissioned to illustrate a book called *The London Child*, by Evelyn Sharp, Miss Garnett's family background was middle class, and she was 'appalled by conditions prevailing in the poorer quarters of the world's richest city', as London was then. The level of poverty was a terrible shock and she determined to use her talents to do something about this situation.

The best-known result of this decision is *The Family from One End Street*, which is firmly based on Miss Garnett's first-hand experiences in London at the time. But the fame of the book is due to the fact that it is more a great story, rather than any kind of propaganda about the plight of the poor. It is a timeless classic because it transcends the social conditions which form its background. Countless readers have been moved and amused by the Ruggles family at Number 1, One End Street; but they have all profited from the reading as well.

The setting of the book
several publishers turned

that it was not suitable reading for children! But as soon as it was published, in 1937, it gained the prestigious Carnegie Medal for 1938, beating J. R. R. Tolkien's *The Hobbit* in the process.

Several other books followed, including sequels called *Further Adventures of the Family from One End Street* (1956) and *Holiday at Dew Drop Inn* (1962). Miss Garnett was a seasoned traveller, and was particularly attracted to the frozen north. She once claimed to have crossed the Arctic Circle sixteen times, and she also wrote a well-received book about the eighteenth-century Norwegian explorer Hans Egede.

Some other Puffin Classics to enjoy

PETER PAN   J M Barrie

SELECTED CAUTIONARY VERSE   Hilaire Belloc

ALICE'S ADVENTURES IN WONDERLAND
THROUGH THE LOOKING GLASS
Lewis Carroll

PINOCCHIO   Carlo Collodi

THE LITTLE BOOKROOM   Eleanor Farjeon

KINGS AND QUEENS   Eleanor and Herbert Farjeon
A CHILD'S GARDEN OF VERSES
Robert Louis Stevenson

AT THE BACK OF THE NORTH WIND
THE PRINCESS AND CURDIE
THE PRINCESS AND THE GOBLIN
George MacDonald

WORZEL GUMMIDGE   Barbara Euphan Todd

THE INCREDIBLE ADVENTURES OF PROFESSOR
BRANESTAWM
Norman Hunter

A BOOK OF BOSH   Edward Lear

The Family
from One End Street

AND SOME OF THEIR ADVENTURES
WRITTEN AND ILLUSTRATED BY EVE GARNETT

'*A happy snap at No. 1 One End Street*'

PUFFIN BOOKS

PUFFIN BOOKS

Published by the Penguin Group
Penguin Books Ltd, 27 Wrights Lane, London W8 5TZ, England
Penguin Books USA Inc., 375 Hudson Street, New York, New York 10014, USA
Penguin Books Australia Ltd, Ringwood, Victoria, Australia
Penguin Books Canada Ltd, 10 Alcorn Avenue, Toronto, Ontario, Canada M4V 3B2
Penguin Books (NZ) Ltd, 182–190 Wairau Road, Auckland 10, New Zealand

Penguin Books Ltd, Registered Offices: Harmondsworth, Middlesex, England

First published by Frederick Muller Ltd 1937
Published in Puffin Books 1942
33 35 37 39 40 38 36 34 32

Printed in England by Clays Ltd, St Ives plc
Set in Monotype Baskerville

CONTENTS

ILLUSTRATIONS

8 ILLUSTRATIONS

CHAPTER ONE

The Christenings

MRS RUGGLES was a Washerwoman and her husband was a Dustman. 'Very suitable too,' she would say, though whether this referred to Mr Ruggles himself, or the fact that they both, so to speak, cleaned up after other people, it was hard to decide.

Mr Ruggles's name was Josiah, and he was called Jo for short by his friends. His wife had a variety of names for him – 'Here – Jo', 'Hi – you!', 'Dad', 'Old Man', and, when she was in a *particularly* good temper and sometimes on Sunday afternoons, 'Dearie'.

Mrs Ruggles's name was Rosie and no one, except her children, ever thought of calling her anything else.

There were a great many Ruggles children – boys and girls, and a baby that was really a boy but didn't count either way yet.

The neighbours pitied Jo and Rosie for having such a large family, and called it 'Victorian'; but the Dustman and his wife were proud of their numerous girls and boys, all-growing-up-fine-and-strong-one-behind-the-other-like steps-in-a-ladder, and-able-to-wear-each-others-clothes-right-down-to-the-baby, so that really it was only two sets, girl and boy, summer and winter, Mrs Ruggles had to buy, except *Boots*.

A great deal was heard about boots in the Ruggles household. They were always wearing out and being taken to the little shop round the corner to be 'soled and heeled', and 'tipped' with bits of iron or rubber in order to try and make them last a little longer. Nearly every week one of the little Ruggles could be seen running with a boot in either hand to the shop, or returning with a bulky parcel badly wrapped in old brown paper.

The Ruggles family lived in a small town – that is to say, there were three cinemas and Woolworth's five minutes' walk from their door, but no green fields without a sign of a house and just a hedge and trees all round, unless they walked for half an hour. The Town was called Otwell, except on the Railway Station and in advertisements where it was called 'Otwell-on-the-Ouse'. This was misleading, as many a visitor, lured from London in the summer by posters of the Ouse with Otwell and its famous Castle rising from the banks, had discovered. For, in reality, the Ouse, a muddy sort of stream, flowed through the fields to the sea, six miles off, some way outside the Town; there was one place where it curved in, as if out of curiosity to see what the Town was like, and that was just beyond the station, so that it was really only the Railway Bridge and signal box that could truthfully be said to be 'on the Ouse', and the Railway Company made the most of this.

The Ruggles lived at No. 1 One End Street, which was in the middle part of the Town, nearest Woolworth's and the cinemas and farthest from the fields. From Monday till Friday morning the house, which was very old and very small, was full of steam and the smell of damp and drying clothes, but on Friday afternoon and Saturday it got aired a bit, and by Sunday was as clean and tidy as any other in the Town. Outside hung a blue board on which was painted in large white letters, 'The Ideal Laundry. Careful Hand Work', and underneath, in smaller letters, the mysterious words 'Bag-wash'.

There was a small yard at the back where the washing was hung to dry on fine days, and where Mr Ruggles did a little landscape and kitchen gardening in his spare time, kept three hens in an old soap-box, had dreams of

Running with a boot in either hand

a Pig, and at times, being a Dustman, nightmares of a Sanitary Inspector.

*

Lily Rose was the eldest of the Ruggles family. She was twelve and a half – going on thirteen, and already in the top class but one at school, and handy with the mangle at home. Her great trial in life was her name, for she was a red-haired stoutish child and bore no resemblance to a lily of any kind or a rose either unless it were a cabbage one, but, as she sometimes sighed, she supposed it might have been worse. It might indeed. It nearly *was*!

One day, before they were married, Rosie and Jo went on An-Excursion-to-London. Amongst other places they visited the Tate Gallery where they saw a picture – 'Lovely', to Rosie's way of thinking, and 'That Real', though at the same time confusing. It was called 'Carnation, Lily, Lily, Rose,' and it showed two children among the flowers at dusk engaged in hanging up Japanese lanterns. Rosie was undecided whether the title referred to the flowers or the children; each was spelt with a capital letter, but the actual flowers were rather vague whereas the children were solid enough; but then, why was Lily there twice over and *could* one call a child Carnation? Jo, on being asked, said he didn't rightly know, and for his part was puzzled over the artist's name in the corner – Sargent – and couldn't understand how soldiers got time for that sort of thing though he'd always heard the army were an easy job. 'Spelt it wrong, too,' said Rosie looking more closely. 'It's one of them catch-words. I know. My uncle was in the Police – would have been sergeant himself if he hadn't been caught setting rabbit wires one night – collecting skins to make his wife a nice fur coat, he were – eighty-three they found in the back kitchen. Too kind a man he was – that were *his* trouble.'

Jo, who had heard this story before, said, well it didn't matter anyway, and he'd like to see some more cheerful kind of pictures, so they went into another room and enjoyed battle scenes and shipwrecks; Jo's boots, which had been newly 'tipped', making a great noise on the beautiful shiny floor and causing a lot of annoyed glances from the middle-aged ladies and haughty-looking young artists who seemed to be up for the Excursion too. It was

One End Street

only when they were thoroughly tired after a finish-up at
Madame Tussaud's and the Zoo and a ride on some
swing-boats at a fun fair, and were sitting over fish-and-
chips and cocoa in a tea shop, that Rosie mentioned the
picture again.

'Carnation, Lily, Lily, Rose,' she murmured between
a mouthful of fish-and-chips and rather hot cocoa.

'What is it, Rosie, swallowed a bone?' asked Mr Ruggles sympathetically.

'Bone – not likely – they're filleted – it's that picture.
Jo, when we're married, I'd like to call our first baby
Carnation Lily Rose; it would be after me, and we
could choose Carnation or Lily for first.'

'And what if it's a boy?' asked Jo.

'It won't be,' said Rosie firmly.

It was not; but at the church door Jo protested so

strongly against Carnation as a name for his first-born, and the Vicar said so sternly, 'Come, come; I have three other babies to christen and my wife has friends to tea, you *must* make up your minds,' that Rosie gave way and the screaming red-haired baby was christened, without further argument, simple Lily Rose.

The next baby was a girl too, and Jo said it was his

A thin freckled child with spindly legs and wispy hair

turn to choose a name this time, and she should be called plain Kate after his dear mother.

'Plain *she* may have been,' retorted Rosie, 'but my baby's a beauty; aren't you, lovely?' but alas! Kate justified her name, and plain she grew up, a thin freckled child with spindly legs and wispy hair – a startling contrast to the stout Lily Rose.

Twin boys came next, and Mr Ruggles, who had

called at the Vicarage to ask for kind assistance in clothing his sons, only *one* having been expected, spent the Sunday after their arrival in church. This was partly in order
to be out of the way of the fuss at home which the twins'
arrival had caused, and partly as a kind of compliment
to the Vicar's wife who had been so obliging in the matter of extra baby clothes. For Mr Ruggles was not an

– a startling contrast to the stout Lily Rose

ardent churchgoer, and it had crossed his mind on the
Vicarage doorstep that his last attendance had been at
the Harvest Festival held several months previously.

Although he knelt, stood and sat down with the congregation, Mr Ruggles found it hard to keep his attention on the service, for his mind was busy with many
things. At the present moment the Twins filled most of it,

but one corner, his gardening corner, was very much oc-
cupied with the progress of his spring vegetables and
how it was that Mr Hook at No. 2 One End Street was so
much further on with his leeks and carrots. Then there
was the problem of whether one or two more hens could
be squeezed into the soap-box. If the family was going to
increase at the present rate, thought Mr Ruggles, the
more he could produce in the food line at home the
better. And then, always, of course, there was the Question of the Pig. Here Jo gave himself up to a few moments' happy dreaming. . . . Surely, in that corner between the hen-box and the little tool-shed, there was
room enough for a small sty; he could take in a bit of the
flower border and Rosie could have her clothes line a
few inches shorter – come to that, he might even pull
down the tool-shed altogether and keep his tools in the
kitchen, though no doubt Rosie would object. Anyway,
with twins in the house, it was high time the Pig Question
was really considered seriously. There was a fleeting
vision of the Sanitary Inspector, but it was of the briefest,
and as the congregation sat down for the Second Lesson,
hens, vegetables and twins once more filled Mr Ruggles's
mind.

'Now the names of the twelve apostles are these,' read
the Vicar.

Jo pricked up his ears. Names. There was another
problem. Rosie had been very quiet about the names this
time. He'd said nothing himself, but he was sure she'd
something up her sleeve – he believed she'd never quite
forgiven him over that Carnation business and Kate. It
looked as if he ought to let her have some say in the matter this time, but, really, he drew the line at fancy and
flowery names for boys, and they *would* be fancy or flowery or both if Rosie had a hand in it he was sure.

'Simon who is called Peter and Andrew his brother,' read the Vicar, 'James the son of Zebedee and John his brother, Philip and Bartholomew, Thomas and Matthew . . .'

'Seems to go in pairs like,' said Jo to himself. It seemed encouraging. 'Better pick two of these and get it over,' he thought, but the Vicar was reading on, and the next thing Jo caught was about a workman being worthy of his meat and that, too, he felt, was singularly appropriate and hoped his Sunday dinner would be a good one! Then, as if an idea had suddenly struck him, he seized a prayer book from the ledge in front of him, and, after wetting his finger and rustling many pages, found the place he wanted. He pulled a stub of pencil from his pocket, held it poised over the list of the apostles, shut his eyes and brought it down 'plop!' James and John. Jo breathed a sigh of relief – he'd been afraid of Philip and Bartholomew – especially Bartholomew. 'That decides it,' he muttered, and Mrs Chips, the grocer's wife, sitting resplendent in sapphire blue velvet in the farthest corner of the pew so that no one by any possible chance should think they were friends (so great is the gulf between grocery and scavenging), turned a stern and reproving eye on him. But Mr Ruggles was oblivious; a problem was solved, and his mind made up for him – a labour-saving device he much appreciated. The Twins' names were settled, and he would slip round to the vestry immediately after the service and arrange for the christening.

When he got home with the good news Rosie was annoyed. 'Decided, have you? Well, I've decided too; Roland and Nigel – that's what they're going to be. James and John indeed!'

'*Roland and Nigel* – what*ever*!' exclaimed Mr Ruggles. 'Not if I know it – a dustman's sons!'

'And what's wrong with dustmen?' retorted Rosie – 'where'd people be in *this* Town, I'd like to know, if it wasn't for you – and me too for that matter – washing for them and cleaning up after them – a fine state they'd be in!'

'Maybe,' said Jo, 'but I won't have my sons called Roland and Nigel, and besides, I've just told you, I've given the names to the Vicar.'

'Well, you can go and tell him you've changed your mind, that's all, and now for goodness' sake go and let the hens out – you forgot 'em this morning.'

But once again Jo had his way. Rosie was tied with two babies at once to look after – not to mention Lily Rose and Kate, and after all ... Roland and Nigel ... perhaps ... the other kids might laugh at them; she was always glad (though secretly) they'd knocked the Carnation off Lily Rose. She got ragged as it was, now she'd begun to go to school ...

The Twins were christened James and John.

For two years there were no further additions to the Ruggles family, and then another boy appeared. 'There'll be no difficulty about this one,' said Jo. 'He'll be called after me.' He was, but there was a difficulty all the same. Two 'Jo's' in one house caused so much confusion that Mr Ruggles had to become 'Old Jo', and sometimes, when he was tired, he said he felt it.

Another two years went by before the next baby came, and this time it was a girl. 'Good thing too,' said Mrs Ruggles, 'I'm tired of boys. And it's my turn to choose a name,' she continued, looking hard at Old Jo as he sat smoking his after-tea pipe. 'Yes, it's my turn, and I'm going to have my way this time. "Margaret Rosie" she's going to be, after me and the little princess mixed, and if that's too grand for a dustman's child – well, you can always call her Peggy – I shan't object.' She had her way, although Mr Ruggles pointed out she already had one child called after her, and the baby was christened Margaret Rosie and very shortly became Peggy, and before she was two years old, Peg. It seemed, too, she was to remain the youngest of the Ruggles, and then, although Mrs Ruggles was tired of boys, four years later another one appeared. 'And the last I hope, girl or boy,' said Rosie.

There was less arguing than usual over this baby's name, for Rosie had a bright idea and suggested it might be rather nice and a delicate compliment to call him after the Vicar who had so kindly, free of all charge, christened the first half-dozen. 'Depends on what his name *is*,' said Mr Ruggles guardedly. (He had fears of Roland or Nigel or something like them again.)

Although Mrs Ruggles was not the regular laundry woman for the Vicarage, she occasionally did odd work to 'oblige' Mrs Theobald, the Vicar's wife; and one evening when she was returning some of her obliging work she decided to ask the Vicar if he would mind if she called her last baby after him.

The Reverend Theobald said he would be delighted, but his name was James, and surely, if he was not mistaken, had not that already been bestowed on one of the twins – would William, his second name, do?

Mrs Ruggles said, oh yes, it would do very well indeed, thank you, and was just going to add that her husband couldn't say there was anything wrong with *that* for a dustman's son, when it occurred to her that perhaps it wouldn't be very tactful and . . . what was he saying . . . A great expense so many children . . . and here was a pound note . . . a christening present for William.

Mrs Ruggles almost ran back to No. 1 One End Street with the good news.

'Well?' said her husband as he met her at the door and took her empty laundry basket, 'well, what have you done about it? His name's James – I've just seen it in the Parish Magazine – but there was a W too,' he added hopefully.

'A "flowery" name,' cried Rosie, rushing across to the cradle, and lifting the sleeping baby in her arms and kissing him so that he woke and howled dismally. '*Another* "flowery" name!'

'*What?*' cried Jo. 'Come off it; I won't have no Carnations and such like in my family – and a boy too!'

'He's William!' shouted Rosie, 'Sweet William, and he is sweet too, and he's give me a pound note for William for a christening present!'

When, at last, Mr Ruggles disentangled the 'he's' and the 'Williams', he breathed a sigh of relief.

So the baby was William, though not always sweet; and he was the last.

CHAPTER TWO

Lily Rose and the Green Silk Petticoat

LILY ROSE, as has already been said, was Helpful in the Home. She could wash and mangle fairly well, scrub steps, knew how to fry bacon-and-eggs and kippers, and was an expert at blowing the noses and scrubbing the ears of her young brothers and sisters. Her great ambition was to own a laundry too – not a 'hand' affair like her mother's, but a real steam one where she would walk about and tell dozens of girls in white overalls how to work. When she was not doing this, she would be showing visitors round or sitting in an office writing letters to the customers to explain why such a tired-looking handkerchief had been returned in place of their nice linen one with an embroidered initial in the corner. (Lily Rose knew all about this kind of correspondence – her mother did a lot of it.)

One afternoon, a pipe having burst and flooded her classroom, Lily Rose came home early from school. The

An expert at scrubbing the ears of her younger brothers and sisters

front door was shut and locked, so evidently her mother and the two youngest children were out. She found the key in its usual place under a broken brick on the second step, and went in.

It was ironing day and piles of ironed and unironed garments lay about. The house linen – sheets and towels and things – seemed to be finished and were piled up in heaps ready to be aired.

So far Lily Rose's ironing activities on customers' washing had been confined to these dull and easy goods, though she had often tried her hand, not always very successfully, on her own and the family's clothes. The brilliant thought occurred to her that it would be an excellent idea and also her 'good deed' for the day (she was a Girl Guide) if she were to finish off the ironing by the time her mother returned. It would be a lovely surprise, and at the same time a way of showing what she could do once she really had a free hand.

The irons were heating on the fire, and Lily Rose, without further hesitation, threw off her hat and coat, rolled up her sleeves, spread out a garment on the ironing blanket and seized one. Forgetting the stand, she put the iron down for a moment on the ironing sheet. Immediately a rich smell of burning blanket filled the room, and Lily Rose was sorry to see a large smouldering hole. She hastily put the iron on the stand and waited patiently for it to cool, testing the heat at intervals by the simple and professional method of spitting on her finger and dabbing it quickly on the iron. After some minutes of this she decided the iron was ready and set to work on a baby's overall. She made quite a good job of this and hung it proudly over a chairback to air, and, encouraged by such success, embarked upon the next garment – a green artificial silk petticoat. Now Lily Rose had heard much talk about the difficulties and dangers of ironing artificial silk, and, although she had never attempted such a thing before, she was not deterred; the great thing, she knew, was not to have too hot an iron. She spread out the petticoat carefully, took what she thought to be the cool iron from the stove and began. She made one long sweep up and down with the iron, and oh! what was happening! The petticoat was shrinking . . . shrinking . . . shrivelling up . . .

running away before her eyes! Smaller and smaller it grew, while Lily Rose gazed fascinated and as if rooted to the spot, her eyes and mouth round 'o's' of horror!

At last the shrinking seemed to stop and there it lay, the beautiful green silk petticoat, no bigger than a doll's – too small even for William – had he worn such things!

Poor Lily Rose! The smoking iron-holder in her hand

Lily Rose sat down on a pile of airing sheets and wept!

soon told her that she had taken the hot iron from the fire by mistake, and, of course, artificial silk – ! Lily Rose put the iron back on the fire, sat down on a pile of airing sheets and wept!

Five minutes later the door opened and in came Mrs Ruggles with William in her arms and Peg hanging on to her skirt. 'Goodness gracious, what a smell of burning!' she cried, 'something's scorching!' and then, catching sight of the tearful Lily Rose: 'What you here so early for

– been sent home from school? – In my day we got kept *in* not let *out*.' Then, as Lily Rose made no reply, 'You're not *hurt*?'

But Lily Rose was past speech; she could only point to the table where the remains of the petticoat lay.

'Whatever *is* the matter?' cried Mrs Ruggles. 'Speak, do. I can see you've been and burnt my ironing blanket, anyway, and what's this thing?' she added, going up to the table. 'Doll's clothes? *How often have I told you not to touch the irons when I'm out!*'

'It's not doll's clothes,' wept Lily Rose, now very tearful indeed. 'It's a customer's petticoat; we was all sent home early (sniff) because there was a flood (sniff), and I was trying to help you and do my good deed for the day (sniff) for the Guides (several sniffs).'

Mrs Ruggles was very angry. Although she lost handkerchiefs and *did* shrink woollens occasionally, she was a good and careful worker, and in all her long career as a

laundress had certainly never reduced a garment to one-sixth of its original size!

'That petticoat belongs to Mrs Beaseley up at The Laurels in Sycamore Road – one of my best customers, I'd have you know,' she cried. 'Both her children have a clean frock a day each in the summer, and I've given her satisfaction for over three years! It will have to be replaced, and a nice expense *that's* going to be! "Good deed" *in*deed! Well, it don't look like it to me, and I've no patience with these Guides – seems to me Guiding's about the last thing they do. Tomorrow you'll come with me to Mrs Beaseley's and explain as it was you and not your mother, who's a careful, hard-working, reliable laundress, as spoilt her nice petticoat, and she'll have something to say to you, I shouldn't wonder; and you'll get no jam for tea today, and no cake on Sunday neither. Now then, stop that sniffing, put the kettle on and get the tea.'

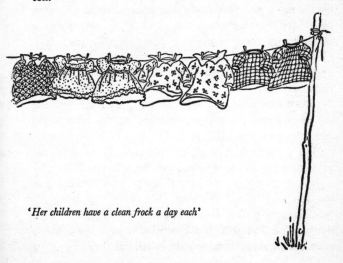

'*Her children have a clean frock a day each*'

The next morning Lily Rose and her mother set off to return Mrs Beaseley's laundry.

If only, thought Lily Rose, it hadn't been Saturday! Then she would have been safe at school. But, instead, here she was, helping her mother, still very cross with her, to carry the laundry basket with one hand, and clasping the remains of the green silk petticoat done up in a parcel in the other. And what she felt like inside – ough! Sick at the very thought of Mrs Beaseley and her house and her fat cook who usually opened the back door to them and made silly remarks. What remarks she'd make today! And Mrs Beaseley herself! Probably she would be going to a party on Sunday and want to wear her beautiful petticoat; perhaps she might even say that Mrs Ruggles must buy her one by this evening, and how awful that would be! Both the twins and Mr Ruggles had had their boots soled this week, and Mr Ruggles's auntie had died and they'd sent a wreath which cost a whole 3s. 6d. – the family funds were very low, she knew. Worse still, perhaps Mrs Beaseley would say Mrs Ruggles needn't wash for her any more after this. And the silly part of it all was that she, Lily Rose, had meant to be so kind and give Mrs Ruggles a surprise. Life was a puzzle, she decided.

At last they reached the house, and Lily Rose, wishing she were dead twice over, knocked at the back door. That fat cook opened it.

'Early today, Mrs Ruggles,' she said. 'Got a helper, I see; come right in and wait a minute, will you?'

Just at that moment Mrs Beaseley herself came into the kitchen. 'Good morning, Mrs Ruggles,' she said, 'you're early today. Is this one of your large family – I don't think I've seen her before? I expect she'd like a glass of lemonade or some cake, wouldn't she?'

'She'd *like* it all right, thank you,' replied Mrs Ruggles, 'but she don't *deserve* it!'

'How's that?' said Mrs Beaseley, turning to Lily Rose, but with such a twinkle in her eye that that young lady felt better at once.

'You tell Mrs Beaseley yourself,' commanded Mrs Ruggles.

'Well, come in and have the cake first, and tell me after,' said Mrs Beaseley. 'Bertha,' she called to the fat cook, 'get a cup of tea for Mrs Ruggles and some cake for the little girl' – she turned to Lily Rose – 'I don't know your name?'

'Please, it's Lily Rose,' said the child shyly – she *hated* telling her name – people so nearly always laughed. But Mrs Beaseley didn't laugh. Surprisingly instead, she said, 'What a pretty name! I don't think anyone with such a nice name could do anything *very* dreadful, do you?' And she smiled so kindly that Lily Rose nearly began to cry again.

'Silly fool I am,' she said to herself, 'she's ever so kind.'

They went into the kitchen, and while Mrs Ruggles drank her tea and Lily Rose ate her cake – she took a good slice for she knew she wasn't going to have any next day at home – Mrs Beaseley asked after Mr Ruggles and the family, and especially the progress of William.

'Grows fine he does,' said Mrs Ruggles, pleased and smiling again at such interest in her family. 'Nurse says he's the best baby at the Welfare Centre – I takes him there once a week to be weighed.'

'You'll have to send him to the baby show in July, Mrs Ruggles,' said Mrs Beaseley.

'Well, *I'd* like to,' said Mrs Ruggles, 'but his father don't hold with them. He gets *Ideas* in his Head, Ruggles does,' she added.

'I'd like to meet your husband, Mrs Ruggles,' laughed Mrs Beaseley. 'I come across so few people with ideas in their heads!'

Lily Rose stared. This was a new way of looking at things. Her own head was always full of ideas – too many it seemed. Yesterday's trouble had been an idea – if only she could explain that to Mrs Beaseley perhaps she wouldn't mind quite so much about her petticoat.

Just then the fat cook returned with the empty laundry basket. 'I'm afraid there's something missing, Mrs Ruggles,' she said. 'There's one green and one pink petticoat on the list, the pink one is here all right – I'm afraid you've forgotten to put in the other.'

Mrs Ruggles looked at Lily Rose, and Lily Rose looked at Mrs Ruggles, while Mrs Beaseley looked inquiringly at them both. 'Please Miss – Madam I mean,' began Lily Rose breathlessly. 'It was an idea (gasp) – I mean I had an idea. I ironed your petticoat to surprise Mum and (gasp), because I'm a Guide and have to do a good deed every day. I didn't mean to spoil it (gasp) – truly I didn't – I used the hot iron by mistake and the stuff ran away soon as I touched it (gasp) – and oh, please, *do* you think you could wear the pink one if you go to a party to-morrow and wait till next week for Mum to get you another (gasp) – because you see Dad and the twins all had their boots soled, and Auntie died (gasp) and we sent a wreath and . . .' thrusting the parcel into Mrs Beaseley's hands, Lily Rose burst into tears.

But when Mrs Beaseley undid the parcel and saw her petticoat *she* burst out laughing. 'I never saw anything so funny!' she cried, 'I should *love* to have seen it running away from the iron – it doesn't matter a bit, Mrs Ruggles. It was a cheap petticoat, and I know artificial silk behaves like that sometimes if the iron is too hot. Cheer up,

Lily Rose. Even if your ideas aren't always a success it's a good thing to have them, and I'm sure you meant to do a good deed. I used to be a Guide once,' she added, 'and I've made lots of mistakes over good deeds in my time. Cheer up now and have some cake and tell me what you're going to do when you leave school?'

There was a long pause. Lily Rose sniffed. 'I want to run a laundry,' she said shyly at last.

Oh, how Mrs Ruggles and Mrs Beaseley laughed, and as to the fat cook, Lily Rose thought she would have a fit! At last she began to giggle herself – did seem a bit of cheek after what she'd done!

'I mean a *steam* laundry,' she said, but they only laughed more.

'Never mind, Lily Rose,' said Mrs Beaseley. 'It's another Idea, and a very good one, but don't practise on my clothes again, will you? And now how about taking home the remains of that cake for the other children, and some of those biscuits for yourself?'

It was a very different journey home! To begin with, Mrs Ruggles was no longer cross – she was laughing. 'You beat all, you do, you and your ideas and your laundry,' she kept saying. And although Lily Rose still held one side of the laundry basket it was empty and light, and instead of the remains of the petticoat in her other hand, she carried the remains of a very good cake and a bag of biscuits. She felt perfectly happy again, and only longing for the evening to tell the story of her good deed and adventures at the weekly Guide meeting. As for the no cake and jam at home, she'd eaten so much she felt she didn't want any more for a week, and anyway, if she did, she'd got the biscuits.

Lily Rose began to sing.

CHAPTER THREE

Kate is Eleven-Plus – and Minus!

IF Kate Ruggles took after the late Mrs Ruggles Senior in looks, she made up for it in intelligence. Mr Ruggles maintained that this, too, was hereditary.

'Wonderful woman, in many ways, my mother,' he would say, while Mrs Ruggles retorted that from all accounts they was queer ways, and for her part she thought Kate's brains came from *her* side of the family, to which Mr Ruggles would reply that he hoped they weren't Albert's variety, and then Mrs Ruggles would say no more, for Albert, her youngest brother, had once been a little *too* clever about something, and the result had been Fourteen Days' Hard Labour. Albert was seldom mentioned at No. 1 One End Street.

Wherever they came from, Kate's brains were certainly very good, and her father and mother, though pleasantly flattered, were not particularly surprised when, having attained the age known in State educational circles as 'eleven-plus' (that year of destiny for all elementary school children with any ambition), she sat for a scholarship, in company with several hundred other children, and passed the written exam ninth out of the whole district! But though her parents were flattered, Mrs Ruggles had misgivings, for a scholarship meant the secondary school, and the secondary school meant clothes – *special* clothes – and for five whole years!

'It's like this, you see, Miss,' she said, happening to meet the head teacher from Kate's school one Saturday morning. 'I'm not one of these mothers what wants their children home and earning at fourteen, just when they're growing most and thoroughly tiresome all round; I'd far rather they was safe in school than working long hours in strange jobs or hanging about the streets with none – it's not *that* – it's the *clothing* of her! Coats and gym-tunics, and special stockings and hats, not to mention boots and shoes – *that's* what it means; no more wearing of her sister's old clothes, but new ones all the time, and from all I've heard the government don't help much toward buying 'em; it 'ud be all very well, Miss, if Kate were our only one, but as you knows we've seven to feed and clothe.'

The teacher knew very well, but she pointed out to Mrs Ruggles that Kate had still to pass the final part of the exam, known as the oral test, which would take place shortly and, if she was successful in this too, Mr Ruggles would receive a form to fill up from the Government, his earnings and expenses would be taken into account, and means provided towards Kate's outfit.

'I know it's difficult, Mrs Ruggles, even with what they *do* give, but I hope you won't refuse the scholarship if she wins one – Kate's a very bright child indeed,' she said. 'I'd like to see her have every chance.' And she added that if Kate did as well in the oral test as she did in the first exam, she might even win one of the money prizes given by a Town Councillor to the children who passed highest from the Otwell schools.

So Mrs Ruggles said, well, she'd wait till it were a certainty, and talk it over again with her husband. Ten days later Kate passed the oral test with ease – third out of the several hundred competitors, and received a guinea from the prize fund. Her photograph appeared in the local paper, and the whole family had sardines and chocolate biscuits for tea to celebrate the event!

Mr Ruggles was delighted, and declared that nothing should stand in the way of Kate's continuing to cultivate the good brains that had been bestowed on her.

'It's easy sittin' there and saying that,' said his wife as they were discussing the matter across the kitchen table after the children had gone to bed. 'But do realize as clothes as *is* clothes will have to be found for Kate for the next five years – not to mention boots and shoes!'

'The government'll do summat towards it,' said Mr Ruggles easily, 'and it'll pay us in the end, mark my words, Rosie. My mother always said –'

'I don't care *what* your mother always said,' replied his wife, '*I* say, government or no government, clothes have got to be found right now straight away; don't matter if Kate's a film star in five years' time, things have to be bought and bills paid *now*. And come to that, I doubt if you *do* get your money back on Kate like you suppose, for what do you think she's going to do with her grand education when she's got it?' Mr Ruggles said he had no idea, but was sure his Kate would choose summat sensible. 'Depends how you look at it,' said Mrs Ruggles. 'Some thinks it's sense, some don't, but all knows *as there's no money in it* – and a strange idea for a Town child I'm sure!'

'Well, what *is* it?' asked Mr Ruggles impatiently.

'*The Land*,' replied Mrs Ruggles in a hollow voice. '*Farming!* Kate says if you want to grow things proper you've got to know how to do it, same as anything else; and all about motor-ploughs and chemicals she talks to me yesterday, and then she says as people always wants food which is true, as we knows only too well, and so she'd never be unemployed, and if the others was they could come and stay with her because on a farm there's always lots to eat. And chief thing of all, she likes to be always out of doors.'

'Like her father,' said Mr Ruggles. 'I've always told you, Rosie, as Kate favoured my side of the family.' But he spoke to empty air, for Rosie, hearing a bleat from William, had run upstairs.

A few days later Mr Ruggles received a letter from the Education Authorities asking whether his daughter was going to take her scholarship, and if so, would he kindly fill up the enclosed form. This document contained the most searching questions regarding Mr Ruggles's private life; questions concerning his wife, his relatives and his children; his earnings; whether he owned, rented, or was buying his house on the instalment system, and many other intimate inquiries. Literary composition was not Mr Ruggles's strong point, but he obstinately refused all assistance, and as soon as supper was cleared away, chivvied his family out of the kitchen, spread the form out on the table, and, rolling up his shirt sleeves, set to work. He finished just in time to catch the last post and assured his wife it had taken more out of him than two days' hard work.

'And you from such a brainy family – well, I never!' said Mrs Ruggles sarcastically.

In three days Mr Ruggles received an answer, in which it appeared that, taking his circumstances into account, the Government would be pleased to grant Kate a free place as far as Education was concerned, but did not feel justified in contributing towards her outfit. And by the same post came a letter from the Secondary School, enclosing a list of requirements for young ladies attending it. If the first letter shook Mr Ruggles's composure, the second staggered him. '*Tennis racket!*' '*Shoebags!*' he read out. 'What *next*!'

And Mrs Ruggles, who had read the letters over his shoulder, replied there was only one thing next as *she* could see, and that was to write and tell the authorities as the scholarship was *off*, because they couldn't afford it, and it was no sense thinking they could. Then Kate wept, and Lily Rose wept in sympathy, and William, not to be outdone, set up a loud wail, and soon, between worry and annoyance, Mrs Ruggles was almost weeping too.

Mr Ruggles shut the window for fear the neighbours might hear and think he was ill-treating them, then patting them all on the backs he said to do nothing about it till he came home in the evening; he was sure there was a mistake somewhere, and during the day he might have an idea. And putting the letters in his pocket, he went off to work.

In the meantime, however, somebody else had had an idea, and no less a person than Mrs Beaseley's fat cook! She had seen Kate's photograph in the paper and congratulated Mrs Ruggles when she called with the laundry that afternoon.

'I showed it to Mrs Beaseley, I did!' she cried excitedly oblivious of Mrs Ruggles's forlorn expression, 'and she were ever so interested – sorry it wasn't your Lily Rose!' and the fat cook chuckled. 'But she says to me, she says, "however will Mrs Ruggles afford the clothes and all for that school – do they give money with these scholarships?" "Dear knows!" I says. "Well, you tell her when she calls," she says, "that if any gym tunics and blouses is useful to her I can give her all as Miss Helen grows out of" (that's her niece what spends her holidays here – big girl she is, Mrs Ruggles – make two of your Kate – but you could cut 'em down), so I says I'll tell you and you're to let her know.'

Mrs Ruggles wrung the fat cook's hand and nearly wept again, but this time with relief, and she hurried home as quickly as possible to impart the good news to her husband, for though she was sure he might have made a mistake, she was not so sure he might have had an idea. There he was, however, home already, standing on the doorstep with his hands in his pockets and his face one large beam.

'All's well, Rosie!' he cried. 'It's all a mistake, and a funny one too – you listen!' Mrs Ruggles listened. 'I called at the school dinner time,' continued her husband. 'Seems Kate had told the teacher what had happened, and up she went to the Town Hall to say there must be a mistake; and there *were*!' Mr Ruggles paused impressively. 'It seems,' he went on, 'as I made a mistake about how many children I'd got!'

'*What!*' said Mrs Ruggles incredulously.

Mr Ruggles nodded. 'It seems,' he repeated, 'as I made a seven what looked like a one! You're right, Rosie,' he added, smiling rather sheepishly, 'I'm no scholar! But it'll be *all right*, you'll see!'

It was all right. Mr Ruggles filled in another form, and the Government replied they would be pleased to provide towards Kate's outfit some time in the next six months.

'Which means,' said Mrs Ruggles, 'as the money comes after the clothes has to be bought, and we begins collecting 'em now, even if it it is only May and Kate don't have to start till September.' And taking the bottle of ink off the dresser, and a sheet of her best professional Woolworth-printed note-paper from under the cushion in the wicker arm-chair, she sat down and wrote a letter to Mrs Beaseley saying she would be very grateful for her niece's old clothes any time they could be spared. With them and the guinea Kate had won, they could manage for the present, tennis racket, shoebags and all.

*

Kate Ruggles was so used to wearing her sister's cast off garments, that Mrs Beaseley's niece's things seemed like quite new clothes, and she enthusiastically turned the handle of the sewing machine, while Mrs Ruggles took in seams and turned up 'good' four inch hems on gym tunics, and helped her mother to pack others neatly in brown paper to be put away until she should grow to them. 'Not as you ever really will, as I can see, skinny little flint that you are!' said Mrs Ruggles.

It was thrilling to have so many new clothes all to oneself! Gym tunics, dark red blouses (Mrs Beaseley's niece's white ones dyed with 'Drummer'), and a dark blue blazer with a pocket on which was embroidered a crest, the words Otwell Central School, and a motto in a strange tongue Kate said was Latin, and which she would shortly 'know'. But best of all were the new school hat with a striped band, and the striped school tie to match, which together cost a whole eight and eleven-pence and had to be bought at a special shop! 'Last you till you leave, they'll have to,' said Mrs Ruggles, and Kate felt she wouldn't mind if they lasted for life and longed for the day when the new school would open and she would set forth from home clad in all this glorious array. However, the day was still far distant, and in the meantime the clothes were put carefully away in the chest of drawers in Mrs Ruggles's bedroom, and Kate would steal in when her mother and the other children were out, open the drawer and peep at them. She would take out the velour hat with the striped band and stroke it lovingly, or try again to make out the motto on the blazer pocket. More often she would just sit back on her heels gazing at them, lost in a daydream . . . Would she hate the new school after all? . . . there would be things like 'homework' – however would one do that in the noisy kitchen in the evening, and up here, in the winter, it would be dreadfully cold . . . And all those new child-

She would sit back on her heels, lost in a daydream

ren, who knew such lots more than she did! Well, they soon *wouldn't*, anyway! This would lead her thoughts in a new direction, and she would begin dreaming about Latin and geometry and things they didn't 'do' at the Council school, and of somehow, some day, going to a big College-Place where one learnt to grow corn and potatoes, to milk cows, to mind horses and pigs, and to drive tractors, *properly* . . . and between her and the open drawer she would see the picture of a big farm – like the one out to Swanbury on the London road, surrounded by haystacks and cornstacks, and herself in the middle in some strange way simultaneously making butter and driving a tractor! . . . These dreams would be interrupted by the sound of Mrs Ruggles turning the front door key,

and Kate would hurriedly close the drawer, skip noise-
lessly out of her mother's room and make a great clatter
in her own.

*

One morning, about a week before the new school
opened, while Lily Rose and Kate were helping their
mother to wash up the breakfast things, there was a
knock at the kitchen door. Kate opened it and was surprised to see a school friend, Miss Patricia Watkins, on
the doorstep. During the last three weeks this Miss Watkins had become something of a celebrity; a halo of ro-
mance surrounded her, for her father, the owner of the
newspaper and tobacco shop in the next street, overcome
one day by the entreaties of a Sunday paper, had fallen a
victim to the Competition Habit, and after six years'
wrestling with Cross Words, Picture Puzzles, Fashion,
Football and Racing Forecasts, had succeeded in being
the only entrant to select, in their correct order, the six
most popular jumpers in a Two-Hundred-Pounds-Must
Be-Won Favourite Fashion Contest!

A representative of the newspaper had called in person
and offered him his choice of a bungalow, a motor-car or
a cheque, and Mr Watkins – wisely or unwisely – opin-
ions differed in One End Street – plumped for the cheque
and promptly invested most of it in the better education
of his daughter. This proceeding called forth much comment among his neighbours, while one lady went so far as
to declare that, in her opinion, the whole business was
'fishy', Mr Watkins as a retailer of newspapers being in
touch with their Editors, and therefore liable to receive
what she called 'inside information' which Mr Ruggles,
who was a friend and regular customer of Mr Watkins,
said put him in mind of a disease! However, fishy or not,

Mr Watkins's cheque was banked and his daughter entered for the secondary school, and there she stood, arrayed in all the glory of its uniform, gym tunic, blazer and school hat complete, on the Ruggles's doorstep, inviting Kate Ruggles to an outing at the sea. Her mother and three other girls from school were coming, and her uncle, Mr Sid Watkins, who drove a lorry and would be delivering a load Salthaven way, would take them, leave them on the beach and pick them up on his way home at five o'clock. Would Kate like to come? There was no doubt about that; Mrs Ruggles gave her consent readily enough, and after arranging with Kate to join the party at the shop at eleven, Patricia ran off home.

Kate returned to the washing up and promptly broke the spout off the tea-pot in her excitement. Mrs Ruggles was annoyed, and Lily Rose, who was feeling offended at not being asked to the party too, told her sister she was a clumsy mutt; but Kate was far away, imagining the splendours of Salthaven, and paid no attention to either of them, and five minutes later – smash – went a tea cup!

Mrs Ruggles was still more annoyed, and an hour later, when Kate, having been sent to tidy herself up for the party, demanded her new school clothes from the sacred chest of drawers, she was very annoyed *indeed*.

'What next, I should like to know!' she cried. 'You knows well enough as those clothes is for school and school only – the idea – playing about on a dirty beach and getting salt water all over them! Now don't argue with me,' she continued, as Kate ventured a remark, 'you knows by this time that when I says "no", I *means* "no". If Mrs Watkins lets Patricia wear her new school clothes to a picnic it's no affair of mine – nor yours neither. You wears what I tells you or you don't go at all,' and taking a clean cotton dress which was airing on the clothes line, Mrs Ruggles handed it to her daughter, and without further comment, disappeared into the back yard. Kate took the dress in silence and went slowly upstairs. She was a long time at her dressing, and when she came down she peeped cautiously round the kitchen door before entering. The kitchen was empty. Looking through the window into the yard, she saw William asleep in his pram, Peg making mud pies in the corner by the hens, and Mrs Ruggles busy in the wash house. Lily Rose seemed to have disappeared. The coast was clear, and Kate drew from behind her back, her new velour hat with the beautiful striped school band, and put it on! After all, she argued to herself, it had been paid for with *her* money, it was *her* hat and if she wanted to wear it, well she was just *going* to. She opened the front door and slipped out.

'You'll cop it!' said a voice from above and, looking up, she saw Lily Rose at the window.

'I don't care!' said Kate. 'It's *my* hat!' and, pausing just long enough to make a face at her sister, she ran off at top speed down One End Street.

*

Although it was only six miles away, it was over a year since Kate had seen the sea – last August Bank Holiday to be exact – and in all her eleven-plus years she had never been so far as Salthaven. Mr Watkins's lorry was perfect, and the arrangement by which his sister-in-law, Mrs Watkins, sat in front with him, while the five children rolled and bumped about like corks, and giggled themselves nearly sick in the back, left nothing to be desired. The sun shone, and everything was lovely. Mr Watkins left them at a secluded piece of beach, about a mile from the Town and, after stuffing them well with ham-sandwiches and bananas, Mrs Watkins, who was a very easy-going lady, satisfied herself that the tide was going out, settled herself comfortably against a break-water with a bag of bulls' eyes and her knitting. This knitting was a very absorbing occupation, for Mrs Watkins had caught the Competition Habit from her husband, and encouraged by his success, was engaged in competing for the best hand-knitted baby's dress, made with Mr Somebody's super knitting yarn, in an All Eng-

They started to work off the ham and bananas

land Mammoth Knitting Competition For Mothers. 'Keep where I can see you, and don't do nothing foolish,' she commanded, and popping a bull's eye into her mouth, and fixing her eyes on the book of instructions, she set to work.

She was certainly the ideal chaperone! The children did exactly as they pleased, and started to work off the ham and bananas by attempting to stand on their heads and walk on their hands – not easy feats on a steep and pebbly beach! Patricia's new blazer was finally called into use as a kind of mat to make things easier, and when Kate observed it later in the afternoon, she admitted secretly that perhaps it *was* just as well Mrs Ruggles had said 'no' about hers!

The sea was calm but paddling unpleasant, for the water was chilly and the pebbles hurt their feet, and was soon abandoned in favour of daring each other to walk along the narrow top of a breakwater. This breakwater was slippy at the end with green weed, and the water deep on one side, and it was disappointing when everyone accomplished the journey safely. In about an hour's time Mrs Watkins looked up from her knitting for a moment; there they all were, good as gold, laid out in a row sun-bathing ... *so* good for them ... 'knit three, purl one,' murmured Mrs Watkins, and helped herself to another bull's eye.

'The boat'll be here in half an hour,' presently announced Miss Watkins, consulting her wrist watch (her outfit was complete to the smallest detail).

'*What* boat?' demanded Kate.

'Why, the Channel Boat, what goes back and forward to France, of course,' replied Patricia scornfully – 'they come past here to Salthaven – haven't you never seen them?' Kate was forced to admit she had not, and it was consoling to find that none of the others had either. 'They make a lovely wash,' continued Patricia, 'pity it's not rough, then the waves come right up the beach.'

'Let's make a big heap of stones, and stand on it when the wash comes,' suggested Kate, and everyone agreeing, they set to work with great enthusiasm. It was warm work and Kate was really glad not to be wearing a thick winter gym tunic. Her velour hat was very hot, and after a little while she could bear it no longer – anyway, everyone had had a good look at it by this time – so she ran over and placed it beside Mrs Watkins.

'Purl three,' said Mrs Watkins nodding absently.

They worked rapidly, and by the time the boat was due had built quite a high mound. Patricia explained that the wash would not come until a few minutes after the boat had gone by, and as soon as she had passed they all climbed on to the mound and waited expectantly. Very soon the first wave broke, it was quite small, but behind it came a bigger one and very quickly in succession, three more, bigger still. The mound was surrounded and the children, all clinging together, kept their footing with difficulty on the shifting pebbles as the receding waves sucked them back.

'They're not big waves at all today,' said Patricia disappointedly, but she spoke too soon. The last and biggest wave of the wash suddenly joined forces with an ordinary wave, a rush of water swirled up the beach, demolished the mound completely and plunged them all, stumbling and hurting their feet on the shifting stones, well over their knees in water. But all this was as nothing compared with the sad plight of Mrs Watkins! Happily murmuring 'purl, plain, purl,' she had glanced up to see what the children were doing, and beheld the sea, which she had supposed going out, advancing in a huge wave towards her! Before she could get to her feet, the water was up to her, under her, over her, all round her, and receding again, taking with it her knitting instructions, most of the tea, and Kate Ruggles's precious hat!

The children came running over at her screams as fast as their bare and bruised feet would allow them, and bravely paddled in after the floating belongings. The knitting book was retrieved, and with much difficulty a bag of bread and butter, very much the worse for sea water, but Kate's hat, in company with a cardboard box of cream buns, went floating gaily out to sea! Kate would have plunged in after it, clothes and all, had not Mrs

Watkins held her firmly by both hands. The hat was already floating well out of her depth; there was no possibility of getting it except from a boat, and no boat, alas, was in sight. Kate threw herself on the beach and wept bitterly. Not only was she terribly upset about losing her hat, but terribly alarmed at the prospect of Mrs Ruggles's wrath at home. Mrs Watkins did her best at consolation.

'Look at *me*, now,' she cried, 'wet nearly to me waist – however I'll get dry I don't know, and all the pages of me knitting book stuck together, and those cream buns as I'd brought for your teas floating out there to the fishes?'

That was all very well, but wet or not, Mrs Watkins hadn't got to face an angry mother when she got home; at the same time, there was something grimly humorous in the idea of the fishes eating their cream buns, and Kate tried to stop weeping, smile, and presently enjoy some tea from a thermos which had escaped the deluge, and some salty bread and butter which had *not*. But it was no good; her tears kept dropping into her tea cup and adding to the saltiness of the bread and butter, while, to make matters worse, her hat remained bobbing up and down in front of them, about ten yards out on the water. Why, oh why, didn't a man in a boat come along, or even a bather who could swim out and save it! But no one came; and as soon as the others had finished eating, Kate climbed on to the breakwater, where she sat, vainly scanning the sea for a sail or a swimmer, the hat drifting slowly farther and farther out, until Mr Watkins called with his lorry to take them home, when it was a tiny speck in the far distance.

Mr Watkins was rather inclined to consider the whole adventure as a roaring joke, but, when he saw how unhappy Kate looked and what gloom seemed to have fallen on the party, he took the matter more seriously, and stopping in Salthaven, good-naturedly purchased a fresh consignment of cream buns, which he handed to Kate with instructions to 'cheer-up'. But Kate was quite unable to eat a cream bun; the very sight of them, combined with the thought of her lost hat, and the smell of fish manure with which Mr Watkins had now loaded his lorry, made her feel quite ill. The way, which had appeared so short coming, seemed endless going home. The other children ate the buns and giggled a little, but Kate's sniffs and the fish manure cast an air of depression over the party, and nobody seemed sorry when the lorry drew up at the shop door and they all got out and said good-bye.

Kate walked slowly home wondering how to break the awful news to Mrs Ruggles, and hoping that, as it was Friday, she might perhaps be out delivering laundry, and the dreadful moment postponed. Mrs Ruggles *was* out, but when she returned half an hour later, there was no need to tell the tragic tale, for Mrs Ruggles had met Mrs Watkins on her way home, *and knew it*!

*

In five days, the new school would open, and Kate Ruggles — clever Kate Ruggles who had won a scholarship — was minus a hat! Oh, it was awful! Moreover, the word 'hat' could hardly be mentioned at No. 1 One End Street, and it was extraordinary how, when you didn't dare mention a word, it was the one word you seemed unable to do without! But far worse, was the problem of how to do without a school hat; they cost six and elevenpence, and Kate had only five shillings left of her prize money, and she wanted that for *ever* so many things.

'You'll buy a school band for two shillings, and put it on your old hat, that's what you'll do,' said Mrs Ruggles, 'and it's no good telling me as your old hat's navy and the school hat is black, because I knows it, and it'll serve you right to look different from the others, for it's different you certainly are and no mistake, and beat any child I knows for naughtiness.'

It was useless to argue, even if one had felt like it, but Kate was quite sure she could never, never survive making her first appearance at the new school in a blue hat, when everyone else was wearing a black one! If *only* she could find or make one and elevenpence by next Wednesday and buy another! She wandered aimlessly down One End Street and up into the Town, turning possible and impossible schemes over and over in her head. Half an hour later, gazing idly into a large fruit shop wondering what to do next, two boys whom she knew slightly at school pushed past her, with baskets on their arms, and disappeared into the shop. Kate peeped inside out of sheer curiosity to see what was in the baskets. Mushrooms! Beautiful, fresh mushrooms! Coo! she'd got an idea! As he came out, she caught the elder of the boys by the sleeve. 'Where did you get those, Ted!' she asked breathlessly.

'Ah! wouldn't *you* like to know,' said Ted teasingly. 'Hi, Bill!' he called to his brother, 'here's Kate Ruggles, what knows everything, wants to know where we gets our mushrooms!'

Bill regarded Kate in silence for a moment, then a broad grin spread over his face. 'You get up early, and look for yourself,' he said, and they both laughed and ran off shaking the empty baskets at her as they went.

Rude pigs boys were, thought Kate, but she'd be even with them, and screwing up her courage she went into the shop and asked the young lady in charge how much the mushrooms were. The young lady said, a shilling a pound, and did she want to sell some? Kate said yes, if

she could find any – Coo! a *shilling a pound*! 'These come
London Road way I think,' said the young lady. 'We
could do with some Monday if you liked to bring them
in.'

'London Road way.' It was vague, but Kate had
made up her mind. She must get up very, very early –
long before those two pigs of boys would be out, and
search the fields round that big farm that she always ad-
mired so much, on the London Road. The farm of her
dreams! She was *sure*, somehow, that was the place!

*

'Whatever are you doing of?' demanded Lily Rose
from her side of the bed as Kate was preparing to get in
on hers that evening. For answer, Kate blew out the
candle, for what she was doing was putting their hair
brush beneath the sheet on her side so that its prickles
might waken her every time she turned over in the night,
and prevent any danger of over-sleeping, for tomorrow
the alarm would be silent, it was Sunday, and the Ruggles family 'lay in' late. She fell asleep very quickly, and
must have remained stationary until four a.m., when the
prickly brush awoke her. It was pitch dark, and rather
cold, and the idea of mushroom hunting did not seem so
enchanting a prospect as it had yesterday morning. However, Kate was not to be daunted, and she slid out of bed
as quietly as possible, and began putting on her stockings.
Oh, how the boards creaked! Lily Rose would wake at
any moment, not to mention Peg – they never did this in
the daytime, she was sure; there they went again! In her
anxiety to stand quietly on a creaking board on one leg
and put a stocking on the other, all in the pitch darkness,
she over-balanced, and, falling against a chair by the bed,
sent the tin candle-stick which reposed on it spinning on

to the floor! It made a terrific clatter, and Kate crept quietly back into bed holding her breath. Lily Rose turned over but did not awake, while Peg made no sign at all, but a few seconds later the door opened, and Mrs Ruggles, candle in hand, appeared in the opening, demanding in a hoarse whisper whether it were Burglars or Stomach Ache? Receiving no answer, she proceeded to make a tour of inspection with her candle, and finding no burglars, but an upset candle-stick, and her three daughters apparently sleeping peacefully, decided it must have been stomach-ache 'in their sleep', and returned to her own room. Kate sat up in the darkness and considered. No good, she'd never get dressed in the dark without someone hearing; only thing to do was to go to bed in her clothes. Tomorrow was Monday and washing day, the alarm usually went about half past five; if she were to get up, ready dressed then, she'd have lots of time. She kicked off the stocking she'd put on, pushed the brush to the end of the bed, and was soon asleep again, and the next thing she knew Lily Rose was shaking her and asking where their hair brush was, she was *sure* she'd seen it on the dressing-table the night before last!

Sunday passed peacefully; everyone tried hard to avoid mentioning hats, but that evening Kate's great plan was almost discovered, for just when she had taken off her Sunday dress and was trying to put on her everyday one under her nightie – a most complicated proceeding – in came Lily Rose. However, she succeeded undetected and lay down fully dressed except for her shoes. She was awakened in the middle of a very strange dream, in which her missing hat had turned into a large cream bun with a band of mushrooms and herrings, by the shrill blast of Mrs Ruggles's alarm clock. She waited until she heard her mother go downstairs, unlatch the front door, and go out into the back yard for some coals, then she slid carefully out of bed, and with many an anxious glance at Lily Rose and Peg, slipped off her nightie, and taking her shoes in her hand, crept quietly downstairs and out of the front door. As soon as she was safely round the corner from One End Street she sat down on a doorstep and put her shoes on, then, alternately running and walking, she set off in the direction of the London Road. After what seemed eternity, but was really only half an hour, she reached the first fields surrounding the big farm, and, resting for a moment against a gate to get her breath, she saw two figures coming across the fields towards her, two figures with baskets, two figures who, as they came nearer, she recognized as Ted and Bill!

'Mornin', Kate Ruggles! Found us out, have you!' said Ted as they came level with the gate. 'Well, that was clever of you, but not quite clever enough – you're too late – we've not left *one*,' and he pointed to their baskets, overflowing with the most perfect mushrooms!

Bill said nothing but grinned aggravatingly, and opening the gate they both set off down the road, whistling and waving their hands.

Kate said nothing either – there *was* nothing to say – but she felt very small indeed. Was it any use now, going to look – they might have said that on purpose – she was almost sure she saw a white shape gleaming in the middle of the field. She opened the gate and went in. Yes, she was right, it *was* a mushroom, and feeling more cheerful she put it carefully in her basket. But after twenty minutes searching she only found two more, and these were even smaller. She was hesitating whether to try the next field which was overlooked by the farm, and wondering if she might be turned off for trespassing, when suddenly a voice behind her shouted loudly, 'Hi, you!'

Kate gave a jump and turning round saw a man brandishing a stick at her over the gate. 'Come here,' he shouted, and as she stood stock still, 'Come *here*!' again, only louder. Kate went very reluctantly towards him; was she *never* going to have any luck again? Perhaps winning the scholarship had been the end of it – one big prize to last all her life! It was a melancholy thought! 'Hurry up!' cried the man. Kate tried to hurry, but her legs began to feel like legs in a nightmare and would hardly move. 'So it's *you*!' said the man when at last she reached the gate, '*You*, who've been picking my mushrooms these last two weeks! Do you realize you're stealing, or can't you read?' and he pointed with his stick to a small notice board in the hedge by the gate, on which was printed, very clearly, in large letters, 'CULTIVATED MUSHROOMS. TRESPASSERS WILL BE PROSECUTED.'

'Do you know who I am?' he continued – 'I'm the owner of these fields; *now* what have you got to say for yourself!'

'Please,' said Kate, 'it's the first time I've been here; I never saw that board, and I've only got three tiny little mushrooms, look!' and she held up her basket with trembling hands and showed them to him.

The farmer looked at her searchingly. 'But you *would* have picked them, if there'd been any more, wouldn't you?' he asked.

Kate hung her head; wouldn't she just!

'And what were you going to do with them, when you'd got them?' he continued. 'Eat them or sell them?'

'Sell them,' said Kate promptly.

'To buy sweet stuff, I suppose?'

'No,' said Kate, and blushing to the roots of her red hair, she muttered, 'to buy a *hat*!'

'A *hat*!' exclaimed the farmer. (Extraordinary! just like

his wife! 'What are you going to do with the money from
the bees?' 'What are you going to buy for Christmas?' –
always the same answer: 'a hat!' What *was* it about a hat
that appealed so strongly to the feminine mind?)

'Do you often buy hats?' he asked curiously. 'You don't
appear to be wearing one now.' To his astonishment
Kate threw her basket on the ground, buried her face in
her hands, and burst into tears.

She was not quite sure how it happened, but the next
thing she knew, she was sitting perched on the top of the
gate, the farmer beside her, telling him the whole sad
tale, all about her scholarship, her new clothes, her
disastrous day at the sea, and why she was trying to pick
mushrooms in his field. 'But I didn't see that board,
truly I didn't!' she ended, 'I must have been looking at
Ted and Bill.'

'And who may they be?' inquired the farmer.

'Why, the boys who picked all the mush –' began
Kate, and stopped suddenly. Ted and Bill must have
seen that board, they'd been here lots of times – Ted and
Bill *had* been stealing – if the farmer knew who they were
perhaps he'd put them in prison!

'So you knew who'd taken them all the time!' he was
saying. Kate nodded. 'But you're not going to tell, eh?'

'No,' said Kate decidedly.

'Quite right too! Now look here, you come along with
me to the next field and I'll give you some mushrooms to
sell towards buying a hat, but first you've got to promise
me to tell this Ted and Bill, whoever they are, that if they
ever set foot in my fields again, *they're for it.*' Kate promised very readily. Oh, she'd tell 'em all right, and she
wouldn't half enjoy it too! 'Fancy boys like *you*, *stealing*!'
she could hear herself saying.

The next field was white with mushrooms, and in a few

minutes they had filled Kate's basket and one of the farmer's as well. 'Now off you go,' he said, 'and when you
return my basket you can see over the farm and tell me
some more of what you mean to do when *you* go on the land –
it's something to meet a kid that wants to these days –
girl or boy. Good-bye, and remember about those boys.'

*

'I don't think we can do with any more today,' said
the young lady at the fruit shop, when Kate presented
her baskets of mushrooms (which she had left with
Patricia Watkins while she went home to breakfast) a
couple of hours later. 'We've had a lot in this morning
already.'

'But you *promised*!' cried Kate, aghast.

'I never,' said the young lady. 'I said we could do with
some more Monday; well, we've had some more afore
you come. That's not my fault, that's bad luck.'

Bad luck! It was Calamity!

'I'm only teasing you,' said the young lady. 'I'll take
'em, but we can't give you more than sixpence a pound –
how many's here?'

Kate didn't know, and she watched with great anxiety
while the young lady took them in her scarlet-tipped
fingers and put them in the scales.

'Nearly six pounds,' she said. 'I'll give you three shillings, and *we don't want no more tomorrow*, d'you hear?'

Yes, Kate heard – vaguely – she was busy doing sums
in her head; three shillings and five shillings made eight
shillings . . . school hats cost six and elevenpence . . .

'Here's your money,' said the young lady handing her
half-a-crown and sixpence. 'Now *hop it*!'

And Kate hopped – almost literally – back to One End
Street.

A new hat *and* one and a penny over! One and a penny, one and a penny, one and . . .

'There's - a - parcel - come-for-you-wherever-have-you been-to?' said Mrs Ruggles, when she reached home.

'A parcel for *me*?' said Kate, and taking from her mother a flat narrow package done up in creased brown

'A parcel for me?' said Kate

paper with very knotty string, she tore it open in great excitement. Inside, neatly rolled up, *was her lost hat*! As she unrolled it a piece of paper fluttered out. On it, in very shaky writing was written, in red ink, 'Found out fishing by yours faithfully, Mr J. Putty, 10 Sea Road Cottages, Salthaven,' and underneath someone else had added, in a firmer hand and ordinary ink, 'P.S. Postage would oblige.'

It was staggering! And how far-seeing of the new

school to have insisted on every garment being clearly
marked with its owner's name and address! Except that
this label and the striped band had 'run' a bit, the hat
didn't look much the worse for its wetting. A bit of pres-
sing with the iron, a new band and it would be as good as
ever; certainly there would be no need to buy another,
and as the band would only cost two shillings, Kate was
financially better off than before the disaster – six shillings instead of five to the good! Six shillings to spend instead of one and a penny! She was busy spending them in
imagination when she was interrupted by Mrs Ruggles.

'Out you go,' she commanded, 'to the post office, and
buy a one and sixpenny postal order, and when you gets
back I'll give you a sheet of notepaper and an envelope,
and you sits down and writes to the gent what found
your hat, and sends it him – sixpence for the postage and
a shilling for himself – oh! and you buy a three-halfpenny
stamp as well, and perhaps all that'll *learn* you – tho' I
doubt it.'

But Kate, in spite of the secret money from the mushrooms, had *no doubt about it at all*!

CHAPTER FOUR

The Gang of the Black Hand

JAMES RUGGLES, the elder of the twins, and called Jim
for short, like his father and sisters was afflicted with
Ideas – indeed sometimes, as he himself expressed it, he
was *bursting* with them. He longed to Have Adventure
and See the World, but there seemed little scope at present – Brightwell, six miles off, for the day, was the farthest he had gone from home yet! Lately, however, a
friend had told him about the splendid thriller stories that

could be borrowed free from the Public Library, and after reading about the heroes of these tales and their doings – boys who went whale-hunting or flew round the world in home-made aeroplanes, or twins (Jim took particular interest in this story) who were wrecked on a desert island, lived for a year on coconuts, eventually returning home on a raft with a chest of buried treasure and their fortunes made – after these tales, Otwell seemed indeed a tame place!

'Nuffing ever happens to *me*,' muttered Jim to himself. He said this, half in anger and half as a kind of challenge; had not the heroes in *The Young Explorer* and *The Boy Aviators* said just the same thing and had not adventures by the dozen immediately befallen them?

However, nothing *did* happen to Jim. He got up, ate, went to school, was good or naughty as the mood took him, stood about hoping for adventures, 'despaired' like the heroes of his books (though what this meant he was never quite sure), read more books from the Public Library, ran errands, went to bed, and got up and began all over again; *still* nothing whatever out of the common occurred. No strange-looking men with sacks over their shoulders beckoned mysteriously to him in deserted streets; no old women whose heavy parcels he offered to carry died and left him a hundred pounds. The only old woman he tried to assist told him to 'get along, my dear, your little arms could never manage this heavy load,' and certainly no young man, disguised as a bank-clerk as in *Tony makes Good*, asked Jim to meet him the next moonlight night by the river, turning out to be a cat-burglar, and Jim the very boy in all Otwell his gang needed.

'I'm fed up,' said Jim. 'Nuffing ever happens like in books. I expect I'll stay in Otwell till I die.'

This seemed such a gloomy prospect, especially as it

was Saturday afternoon, that he decided at once to go for
a-walk-by-the-river.

The river was a wonderful place; it breathed adventure! Boats sailed on it, barges from the sea carrying
mysterious freights went up and down (it was tidal for
a little above Otwell). Strange and patient men fished
from its muddy banks, and marigolds and other flowers
in season grew beside it in beautiful squishy mud that was
a delight to walk in. Above all things it was strictly
forbidden by Mrs Ruggles, and therefore doubly attrac-
tive – a sort of adventure in itself!

Even sitting and watching the river was fun. Where did
it come from, where did it go? Jim knew the answer to the
last question – into the docks at Salthaven six miles away
– a place he longed to see beyond all others. Where it
came from he had no idea. He was suddenly struck by his
ignorance of this fact. He brightened up. An Idea! Why
not find out – track the river to its source, right straight
away, now, this very minute! There was an adventure
ready to his hand – *why* had he never thought of it before?

Jim began to run; if he were to finish the job and get
back to supper he had better make haste. He ran past the
little boot shop round the corner, down the next street
and out into the main road to London; past the Park and
Playground where he saw Lily Rose and Kate swinging
each other, John on the Chute and Jo 'minding' Peg in
the Sand Pit (no sign of William); past the cemetery, past
the turning to the Race Course; on and on till he was
quite out of breath. At the allotments he really had to slow
down and there, of course, was Mr Smith from No. 4 One
End Street going in to attend to his cabbages and things.

'You seem in a hurry, young man,' he remarked.

Jim looked at him scornfully and began to run again.
There were fields now and only a few houses. Presently he

Even sitting and watching the river was fun

came to a path where a board said 'To the River only'. He turned down this and was soon in the water-meadows – he could see the river not far ahead.

Hot and exhausted, he stopped and sat down for a moment to get his breath. He looked round him; just ahead was an old lime kiln – he had been in there bird-nesting with John last year. Should he waste time and go in again? It was very late for eggs – still you never knew. He'd found a blackbird's nest end of August last year, and one ought to have 'provisions' on a journey – he'd come away so quickly he'd forgotten to bring anything, and even blackbird's eggs were better than nothing – he and John had eaten a couple each, boiled in an old tin, once, and not been sick. Yes, blackbird's eggs would be a help, he decided.

Jim got up and ran on; time was precious. As he came near the kiln, he thought he heard voices and paused for a minute to listen, but he could hear nothing more and told himself it must have been a cow. At the kiln he slowed up and peeped cautiously in. What he saw made him draw back quickly. He had been partly right after all. He had heard, not *Voices*, but *A Voice*! Inside the kiln, sitting in a semicircle on the floor, their backs towards him, were nine or ten human beings all intently listening to another perched on a wooden box, who was speaking in a low but excited voice. Jim turned to run, but it was too late – he had been seen! He was seized by the arms and dragged into the kiln. He had surprised a secret meeting – a meeting of the Gang of the Black Hand!

*

Jim came home very late for supper that evening and muttered something about bird-nesting to account for it. That night and all the following week he suffered from nightmares of a most alarming description, and would wake shrieking in the middle of the night rousing, not only John who shared his bed, but the entire Ruggles family.

'History – that's what it is!' said Mrs Ruggles after she had been awakened four nights in succession, 'shouting out about daggers and beheadings and pools-of-blood – much more of it and I'll complain at the school!'

Strange to say, John Ruggles, who was in the same 'Standard' as his brother, called out no startling things in *his* sleep, and on hearing his mother's remark at breakfast was beginning to inform her that history lately had been nothing but dates and parliaments and too-dull-for-words, when a kick under the table from Jim stopped him (the twins always understood each other).

Unfortunately John's curiosity was aroused later; when his brother refused to tell him what the kick meant, he was much offended and determined to find out the secret. He worried and worried, buzzing round Jim like some irritating fly. But Jim utterly refused to open his mouth on the subject; for Jim was under an oath – An Oath of Secrecy to the Gang of The Black Hand, and threatened with the most Unspeakable Tortures should he fail to keep it!

*

The Gang of the Black Hand was, in the words of its Captain, Mr Henry Oates aged twelve, son of a foreman at the gasworks, A Dead Secret Society. This did not mean, as one might surmise, that the Society was extinct – a memory – a thing of the past; on the contrary it was very much alive and a flourishing concern! The Gang, or Black Hands, as they called themselves (an appropriate title for most of them), consisted of nine or ten members mostly between eleven and twelve years of age who were sworn to secrecy and liable to most awful and Excruciating Tortures (so awful that they were known only to the Captain himself and written in a small notebook which he always carried in an inner pocket), should they betray the Secrets, Pass Word or any activities of the Society. The Gang met every Saturday afternoon, usually in the old lime kiln, but sometimes behind the gasworks, in a corner of the cemetery or some other quiet spot selected by the Captain. Each member was expected to bring something to eat which he shared among the others, and, whenever possible, a halfpenny or more towards the general funds of the Society. This money was put in an old tobacco tin and buried under a heavy stone in the kiln. Its ultimate use was a little vague, but it was understood to be the correct thing to have, and the members experienced a pleasant thrill each time the tin had to be unearthed to receive a fresh contribution, lest it should have been stolen in the meantime. The real object and excitement of the society, however, were the Adventures each member was expected to 'have' and relate to the others at the Saturday meeting. Whoever was considered to have had the most thrilling was elected Chief Gangster for the coming week, and entitled to an extra share of the rations and much respect. Failure to have an adventure for three weeks running meant dismissal from the next meeting, failure for four weeks, dismissal for a month, and if, at the end of six weeks a member was *still* adventureless, he was Hopeless, No Good to the Gang, and Thrown Out – (literally). The oath, however, remained binding for life – and, of course, the Unspeakable Tortures.

So far (and the Gang had been in existence three months), no one had been such a dud as to have nothing to relate, anyway every second week, and though the standard of the adventures was perhaps a little low – not to say commonplace at times, they passed as such and the horrors of banishment remained unknown.

It was one of the weekly meetings Jim had surprised at the kiln. He had been accused of spying, pinched to make him confess, and after surviving this ordeal without shedding a tear, at last succeeded in convincing the Gang of his innocence. The fact that he, too, had been searching for an adventure when captured rather weighed in his favour, though his idea of tracking the river was dismissed with contempt. Henry Oates had done it two years ago, and anyway, one could now find it all on a local map from Woolworth's – it was no fun. Still, for a kid, it wasn't a bad idea, they supposed.

'Shall we make him a member?' asked the Captain.

Jim beamed. He had no idea what these boys did, but the whole affair breathed adventure, and to be merely associated with big boys like these was a step-up in the world!

Several members objected.

'He's too young'; 'we don't want kids'; 'he'll give us away,' they said.

Jim begged and entreated, gasping for breath in his excitement, and finally it was decided he should be admitted next meeting if it were found he could keep complete silence on the whole subject for a week – if he had an adventure to relate, so much the better, but it would not matter to begin with; the chief necessity was for Absolute Silence and such terrible things were hinted at should Jim breathe One Solitary Word about what he had seen and where he had been that it was no wonder his sleep was disturbed!

During the week, at school and in the streets, boys who had never spoken to him before kept coming up and saying in a threatening whisper, 'Keep yer mouth shut, or–'! Then John's persistent inquiries about the kick were very wearing. Jim began to count the hours till Saturday; only thirty-seven now if one began the day at six. He thought he might just hold out if John would keep quiet. But John would not. 'Shut up,' said Jim furiously at last, 'or I'll give you a black eye!' And as John invariably came off worst in their fights he shut up – temporarily. Well, thought Jim, he was certainly in the thick of an adventure all right, and tried hard to persuade himself it was not rather a mixed kind of pleasure.

At last Saturday afternoon came, and punctually at three o'clock, feeling very nervous, Jim arrived at the kiln.

'Give the Pass Word,' said the Captain, and, although

Jim had been repeating this to himself, several dozen times a day all the week, for one awful moment he found himself unable to remember it! Master Oates looked at him sharply.

'Fresh Fried Kippers,' stammered Jim at last.

'*Herrings*!' said the Captain, scowling at him, 'but you can pass.' Jim passed.

'But it's no good,' he said, after he had given an account of how he had kept silent in spite of John's persistent questionings. 'I couldn't go on another week, anyway; if you has me, he'll have to come too. I talks in my sleep (Jim thought this sounded better than nightmares) and he shares my bed; he hasn't heard anything yet or he wouldn't keep asking, but he *might*; and I'd awful trouble shaking him off coming here,' he added – 'you see we always does things together – we're twins.'

This last statement fortunately appealed to the Captain. Twins were romantic; in the books he read twins invariably came out top; strange adventures befell them, they got mistaken for each other and involved in all kinds of excitement.

'Are you *like*?' he inquired cautiously.

'He's thinner,' said Jim, 'and I got more spots' (by which he meant freckles with which he was covered).

'Ginger hair, both?' pursued the Captain.

Jim nodded.

Finally he was put outside and the matter considered. After much discussion it was decided that if John could be produced that evening, shown to the Gang and approved by them, he could join, but Jim would be held responsible for his brother's silence as well as his own, and the penalty of breaking it – well – Jim knew . . .!

*

Two hours later John Ruggles, to his enormous delight, had been fetched, accepted, and 'sworn in'! Both twins were now members of the Gang. Jim breathed several sighs of relief; sharing the secret with John was quite another matter – exciting with the terror part left out; between them they would defy the World to drag it from them! His nightmares ceased.

'Saturday–no lessons!' said Mrs Ruggles to her husband next morning, 'it'll begin again on Monday – you'll see.'

But Monday night passed peacefully and so did Tuesday and Wednesday and all the rest of the week, and Mrs Ruggles said, well, perhaps it had been Indigestion and not History after all; anyway, she couldn't see there was much to choose between them for giving you horrors and upsetting your sleep.

*

The next thing was to 'have' an adventure and most fortunately, before next Saturday's meeting, there would be a whole holiday from school – an annual event in memory of the founder.

On the holiday morning the twins were so quiet and well behaved at breakfast, that Mrs Ruggles looked suspiciously at them once or twice, and wondered whether it was Mischief or Measles (the latter was said to be about), and determined to keep an eye on them, but while she was speaking to a customer at the door, they had slipped out, and run off down the street, almost before she had realized they were gone. Not Measles, anyway, decided Mrs Ruggles!

Once round the corner of One End Street they parted company – no use having the same adventure – and while John disappeared up the Town, Jim made his way to the river, not near the lime kiln this time, but towards the wharf by the station where the barges loaded and un-loaded. For he had made up his mind last night that he was going to be a stowaway (the Gang of the Black Hand would respect a stowaway even if he *was* a kid!) like the boy in the thriller he had just finished, but with this difference, that while this hero had been gone from home for weeks, Jim was only arranging to go for the day – just down the river to Salthaven where the barges unloaded. The boy in the book had swum across a harbour, and climbed on board a cargo boat while the crew were on shore; Jim could only swim a few strokes, and he was not going to trust himself to the muddy waters of the Ouse; but he was quite sure he would find some way of getting on board a barge.

Two barges were loading at the wharf – one with ce-ment, the other with scrap-iron and drain pipes. There was no one about but the four men belonging to the boats and a mongrel dog asleep on the wharf beside a heap of pipes. Jim walked to the water's edge, inspected the barges and was pleased to overhear one of the men say as he thought they'd be ready to go down on the high tide at one o'clock, all right. This was excellent news! The men would knock off for their dinner at twelve o'clock, and when they came back the stowaway would be, well – a stowaway!

Jim began to feel very excited and wished it were not so long to dinner time! He stood watching the crane swinging sacks of cement on board, until one of the men told him roughly to get out of the way. Feeling rather offended he retreated down the wharf to a heap of sand where he sat keeping an anxious eye on the work for the holds seemed to be filling up rapidly, and this was discon-certing because he had noticed there was nowhere one could possibly hide on the decks! He was wondering what he should do if there was no corner left by the time the barges were due to sail, when a terrific hail-storm broke with great suddenness over the wharf. The men, putting sacks over their heads, ran for shelter to a warehouse, while the dog awoke, jumped to his feet, shook himself, took one look round and, making straight for a drain pipe lying by itself apart from the heap, crawled inside. Jim had no sack, he was some way from the warehouse, and so violent was the hail that he knew he would be soaked before he could reach it. So, jumping off the sand heap, he followed the dog's example, and risking a bitten nose,

Jim crawled in after it

crawled into the drain pipe after it! It was fortunately a friendly animal, hardly more than a puppy, a mixture of many breeds, and wagged a long plumy tail as Jim curled up beside it. The hail beat down for several minutes, than changed to torrential rain and rivulets of water ran past the pipe. Inside, however, it was snug and dry, there was a little straw on the 'floor', and though one could not sit upright, it was comfy enough – comfy enough, Jim decided, in which to go down the river! *Here* was his hiding-place! When the last of these had been put aboard and the men gone to their dinners, he would just walk on to the barge, creep inside one and stay there till they reached Salthaven! What could be simpler? It was almost too good to be true! And coo! *wouldn't* it be summat to tell the Gang!

At last the rain stopped, the dog jumped out, and Jim crawled after him unobserved. A distant clock struck eleven, and feeling rather bored and afraid his continued presence might arouse the men's suspicions, Jim set off for a little walk beside the river, closely followed by the dog, and for the next hour amused himself by throwing sticks and stones for it. As soon as he heard twelve strike, he hurried back to the wharf, delighted to see that all the drain pipes were now on board, and the men putting on their coats. They seemed in no hurry and for one agonizing moment Jim was afraid that perhaps they had decided to eat their dinners in the warehouse in full view of the barges! But no, they were only lighting their pipes, and a minute later, calling the dog, they all walked off towards the town.

As soon as they were well out of sight, Jim hurried to the edge of the wharf, ran up the plank which served as a gangway to the first and larger of the barges and jumped on board. He glanced hastily around, and picking up a sack which was lying near, and selecting the topmost pipe on the pile, he climbed with some difficulty up the heap and crawled inside it. He was just too tall to lie stretched straight out without being seen, but he curled up wrapping the sack round him to keep off the draughts. The round ends of the pipe were like portholes, there was an excellent view each way and it required very little imagination to believe one was in a cabin, bound, not for Salthaven, but the South Seas! Jim had never been so excited in his life – too excited even to feel hungry – (which was as well, for he had nothing to eat and no prospect of getting anything) and doubted whether even Henry Oates himself would be able to beat this!

Very soon the men returned and the two belonging to Jim's barge, which was to tow the other, began starting the engine. All at once, Jim became aware of a strange pattering noise on the pipes, then the sound of sniffing, and suddenly a cold, black nose was thrust into his face!

'Go away!' he whispered, but the dog, delighted to have discovered the kind friend who threw sticks for him, began to utter short, joyful barks! 'Go 'way!' repeated Jim in an agony of fear lest he should be overheard and discovered, but the dog only barked louder. Fortunately, the men were busy with the engine at the far end of the barge, and a few minutes later there was a shrill whistle from the one behind, and a voice cried 'Where's Toni? Hi! Toni!' The dog stopped barking, pricked up his ears, licked Jim's face as if to say good-bye, then obediently scuttled off the drain pipes, leapt down the gangway and up on to the other barge. Phew! Jim whistled under his breath. That *was* a near go! Two minutes later they were off!

*

It was very peaceful lying in the pipe drifting down the river to the soothing thud-thud of the engines. Very soon Otwell was far behind, and they were sailing between water-meadows where horses and cows were grazing. The sun shone, but a sharp breeze blew from the coast, and after half an hour or so, in spite of the sack, Jim began to feel rather chilly and *very* stiff. Presently the water-meadows gave place to marsh land and sea birds flew screaming overhead, the barge began to rock a little, and he judged they must be getting near the mouth of the river. In the far distance he could see houses and factory chimneys and the tall masts of ships. The river curved in and out between the marshes for several miles; it was wider now and the rocking increased. Jim began to feel just a tiny bit sick. This was not at all the correct conduct for a stowaway, and he thought it might be better if he were to shut his eyes for a little while. When he opened them again, the rocking had ceased, and sheds, cranes, and coal dumps stood on the banks. In a few minutes they were entering the first of Salthaven's docks. Very soon they would be at their destination, and Jim began to consider, for the first time, how he was going to get off the barge without being seen; no dinner hour to help this time! On the whole, he decided, he didn't care much if he *was* seen; he had his adventure to relate and even if he got a hiding from the men it was worth it – and the six long miles he'd have to walk home! High walls began to rise on either side, and as the barge was heavily laden and low in the water, Jim found his view was now very limited. Big ships lay at anchor, many with foreign names, their sailors called from them in broken English, and it was most tantalizing to hear and be unable to see them.

All at once the barge seemed to be slowing down, and one of the men passing close to the heap of pipes, shouted to his mates on the boat behind; a minute later there was a bump, somebody whistled and the engines stopped; they had arrived!

But instead of tying up against the dock wall as Jim had expected, they seemed to be tying up beside a big ship! Her enormous sides towered over them – Jim could just see her name, *L'Oiseau-Mouche*, and her port, Havre. Her huge hold lay open, sailors in strange clothes stood expectantly about, and the long arm of a crane hung suspended over it – *waiting*. Jim's heart gave a great leap. He knew, somehow, as plainly as if the sailors had shouted it at him, what that crane was waiting for! It was waiting for cement, waiting for scrap-iron, waiting for drain pipes – *waiting for stowaways!* It was waiting to clutch them on its iron hook and drop them all neatly into the hold of that foreign ship! Quite soon, he, Jim, would be in that hold, scrap-iron, cement, and drain pipes on top of him; somewhere in France, America or Czechoslovakia, his suffocated body would be unloaded. He tried to sit up, forgetting it was impossible in the pipe; *crack* went his head against the earthenware; he flopped back, stunned!

*

Jim lay in his pipe feeling sick and shaky. He knew he must crawl out, shout or do something, but he felt too dazed to move; the noise outside, the shouting, and rattling of cranes, added to his confusion; his wits seemed to have completely deserted him. Now something was tugging at his pipe; now something swung past the opening. A voice cried 'Right away!' and the next thing he knew his pipe, or rather the bundle of pipes of which his was the topmost, was being slowly raised in the air! The sharp breeze seemed to bring him to his senses. Gripping one end of the pipe with all his might, Jim thrust his head out of one end and toes out of the other and, gathering all the breath in his body, let forth a terrific yell! Unfortunately, the wind was blowing strongly, and the cook of a neighbouring ship selected this moment to throw some potato peelings overboard. The gulls, circling overhead on the lookout for food, swept towards it in a screaming mass and Jim's cry was drowned in the clamour; higher and higher they went, swinging right out over the harbour, and before he could collect sufficient breath to utter another, the pipe was hovering over the quay; a minute later he was being gently lowered into the hold of *L'Oiseau-Mouche!*

'*Mais qu'est ce qu'il y a là?*' exclaimed a voice as a sailor
slipped forward to unloose the crane's hook from the rope

Higher and higher they went, swinging right out over the harbour

loop attached to the top pipe. '*Nom de Dieu! C'est un
garçon!*' All of which meant nothing at all to Jim, who
crawled out white and shaking and was promptly and
most unromantically sick over the sailor's feet!

It was perhaps as well that he could not understand the language that followed, nor the threats and curses of an enormous individual who emerged from the depths of the hold clad in a strange sort of blue jumper, and trousers so patched that it was impossible to say which was the original material. After he had shouted himself hoarse, this terrifying person suddenly picked Jim up, and, tucking him under one arm like a parcel, stumped down the gangway, deposited him among a crowd of dock-hands on the quay, and stumped back, still muttering terrible curses on all English urchins.

The men crowded round, staring at Jim as if he had dropped from another planet; where was he from, and how on earth had he come to be in that pipe – while the four on the barges shook their fists at him and shouted furiously to 'beat it quick or it 'ud be the worse for him!' Jim was only too anxious to beat it as quickly as possible, but he felt queer, very queer indeed, everything seemed to be going round in circles and he could only murmur, like a baby, that he wanted to go home.

'Where's home?' somebody asked, and after a bit Jim managed to stammer out 'Otwell'.

'There's a chap here going to Otwell – he'll take you, sonny, cheer up!' And taking Jim by the hand, one of the dockers led him across the quay to where a lorry was standing. Just about to start the engine was no less a person than Mr Watkins-from-the-paper-shop's-brother-Sid!

'Hullo!' he said, 'why, not *another* Ruggles in trouble – and my word if he hasn't half got a bump on his head!'

'He's lucky he hasn't got a broken neck!' said the docker. 'He wants to get back to Otwell; as you seems to know him perhaps you'll take him along? Now remember, you,' he added, swinging Jim up beside the driver's seat, 'no more of your monkey tricks here; you've come off lucky this time, but it won't happen twice. *Do you know*,' he continued, lowering his voice, '*what they do with stow-aways?*' Jim shook his head. 'They give 'em up to the Police!' said the docker impressively. '*That*'s what they do with 'em!' and almost before he had finished speaking Jim caught sight of two policemen approaching the crowd on the quay.

He clutched the docker's hand very tightly. '*Sure* it's lucky this time?' he said.

The docker said yes, he thought so, *this* time, but added (with a wink at Mr Watkins) that perhaps it might be safer to sit out of sight on the floor till they were clear of the docks. Almost before he had finished speaking Jim was off the seat, crouching down beside the gears, and very glad indeed when Mr Watkins climbed into the driver's seat and they started off. He wouldn't feel safe now till he was back in Otwell – perhaps not even then, and when Mr Watkins drew up at the dock gates, and out of a little sentry box, notebook in hand, popped a policeman, his heart nearly stopped beating for the second time that day! However, the policeman seemed entirely concerned with the load in Mr Watkins's lorry and in less than five minutes they were off again, rattling away through Salthaven.

'What you been up to?' inquired Mr Watkins, eyeing Jim curiously as soon as they were through the town and out on the Otwell Road. 'What's all this about a pipe and policeman – been trying smoking?'

Jim was rapidly recovering in the fresh air, and now that all danger seemed over, his spirits were reviving as well. 'I've been *inside* a pipe – all the way from Otwell; I've been a *stowaway*!' he said proudly, 'and I've been awful sick,' he added.

Mr Watkins regarded him uneasily. 'You looks a bit chippy. Don't you be sick here,' he said firmly.

'No,' replied Jim, 'I'm O.K. now. I'm *hungry*–I've had no dinner,' he added plaintively.

'Well I'm not going to feed you,' said Mr Watkins. 'I'm taking no risks, and it'll be tea time when we gets to Otwell, anyway. What did you do it for – swank, or do you belong to a gang?' Jim's heart nearly stopped again! How *could* Mr Watkins have guessed – he hadn't said a word! Mr Watkins did not wait for an answer, instead he remarked reminiscently, 'I used to belong to a gang once – bit older than you I were – The Red Handed Rovers we called ourselves, and we all had to do Daring Deeds – Lord, it do seem years ago!'

'It must be!' said Jim hoping to turn the conversation, but feeling he was treading on dangerous ground. 'You're quite old!'

'Yes,' said Mr Watkins, 'I've turned nineteen,' and he sighed.

'I wish *I* was *nineteen*,' said Jim.

Mr Watkins made no reply. He was recalling the days of his distant youth.

'I wish I was nineteen,' repeated Jim again.

'Well, what 'ud you do if you were?' said Mr Watkins.

Jim hesitated. 'I'd drive a lorry like *you*, Mr Watkins!' he said at last.

Mr Watkins glanced at his passenger, 'Cute kid, aren't you!' he said. And Jim was still wondering what he meant when they drew up near the Town Hall. 'Out you get,' said Mr Watkins; 'take care of that bump you've got, *and don't forget the pass word!* So long!' and laughing at Jim's astonished face, he drove away.

*

Mrs Ruggles was laying the cloth for tea when Jim opened the kitchen door. 'My *word*!' she exclaimed directly she saw him, '*whatever* have you been and done to yourself! I never see such a bump in my life – fetch me a bit of marg. Lily Rose – I can't waste butter on him! Whatever have you been mixed up in – a fight, or a street accident or what! You been hit on the head – well, I'm not blind – who or what hit you – and where's your brother John?' continued Mrs Ruggles without waiting for a reply. 'You don't know nothing about *him* I suppose?' she added sarcastically. Jim could honestly say he did not. 'I *knew*,' continued Mrs Ruggles, rubbing Jim's head gently with the margarine, 'I *knew* there was trouble brewing with you two, this morning. Now you just sit quiet there while I gets the tea, and while you're waiting, read that and then tell me if you still know nothing about where John is! – *and* where you got that bump!'

And to Jim's immense surprise, she put a piece of paper into his hand. Even more surprising, the piece of paper was a telegram – a telegram about John! Jim read it. Kids or not, it seemed the Ruggles twins were going to have summat to tell the Gang all right!

CHAPTER FIVE

The Adventure of the Parked Car

JOHN RUGGLES had a passion for anything which moved quickly on wheels; he knew the make of almost every car on the roads, and most of his spare time was spent hanging around garages and filling stations. He also frequented the large Car Park beneath Otwell Castle, where waiting chauffeurs could sometimes be beguiled into imparting interesting information, or join in a discussion on the merits of the different cars in the Park. Many tourists visited the Castle, and sometimes the remnants of a picnic lunch – a few sandwiches or piece of cake – would come John's way; but best of all was the possibility of being employed to 'mind' one of their cars – how infinitely superior an occupation to minding William! (a very frequent occupation among the elder Ruggles).

One never-to-be-forgotten day this dream had been realized, and for a quarter of an hour, almost visibly swelling with pride, John had stood guard over the very latest in six-cylinder, stream-lined monsters! Even the reward of three cigarette cards (which had seemed hardly to scale) could not dim the glamour of that blissful fifteen minutes! Most decidedly the Car Park was a haunt worthy the consideration of a member of the Gang of the Black Hand, and when the day for adventure dawned, John had no difficulty in deciding where to begin his plan of campaign. As soon as he had parted from his brother at the corner of One End Street, he made straight for it.

It was early when he arrived; there were no tourists about, no cars at all in fact, except a very dilapidated 'Baby Austin' in which sat a large Alsatian dog which growled unpleasantly, and showed such a fine set of teeth as John approached that he retreated hastily to a seat beneath the Castle walls. From time to time he glanced anxiously at the sky. The day, which had begun brilliantly, seemed to be changing; clouds were drifting up and the bushes on the Castle ramparts rustled as if a storm were brewing. He did *hope* it wasn't going to rain – rain would spoil nearly everything! The clock of a neighbouring church struck ten and a few cars began to arrive; John knew most of the owners by sight – a young farmer or two, some civil servants on their way to the Town Hall, and several 'shopping ladies' as he called them, all in a hurry and all scornful of 'minders'! Presently, however, a large Packard, chauffeur-driven, came gliding in and John's spirits rose. Out of it poured five voluble American ladies who decided unanimously that the Castle was Too Romantic and John Too Cute, but they certainly must hustle, and their chauffeur would mind the car, thank you. The chauffeur's expression did not contradict this statement, the ladies hustled off and John moved sadly away. He stood contemplating the Packard at a distance. How the dust showed up on its gleaming dark paint! How marvellous it would be to make a huge J.R. in the middle of that beautiful clear space at the back! But he, John Ruggles, was not such a fool – not with that chauffeur sitting there, anyway. All the same, the temptation was terrific, and he had resolutely to thrust both hands into his trousers' pockets, clutching the linings tightly to keep them there! He was glad when the Americans returned and hustled away. Their place was taken by two young men in a racing car, who asked him the way to the Football Ground and then walked off in the opposite direction. He was busy examining their engine when a very clean, medium-sized grey car drove in. A tall youngish man, followed by a lady, got out.

'Mind your car, sir?' asked John running up.

The gentleman looked at him consideringly, then smiled. 'If you promise to keep your hands off the horn and not write your name in the dust,' he said, and turning to his wife he added, 'We haven't much time, it's nearly eleven now,' and they hurried away in the direction of the Castle.

John smiled to himself. That cove knew a thing or two! ... hands off the horn ... and the dust! Perhaps he worked in a garage ... perhaps he'd even been a minder of cars himself once... One day perhaps he, John, would work in

Heavens! What rain! It was like summat out of a bucket!

a garage and own a car like this! He strutted up and
down, lost in delightful imaginings, indifferent to the
chilly wind that had sprung up and the inky clouds
scudding across the sky. A few drops of rain began to fall,
and then, with the most dramatic suddenness, a cloud
seemed to burst over the Car Park. Heavens! What rain!
It was like summat out of a bucket! John looked wildly
round. No shelter anywhere – he would soon be soaked,
and that would mean going home – probably being com-
mandeered to run messages or mind William – anyway
enormous waste of time. Ugh! now it had turned to hail
and that *hurt*. There seemed to be only one thing to do;

he opened the back door of the car and climbed inside. The seat was piled high with luggage and baskets and bags of food – a most tantalizing smell of fresh fruit and buns was wafting about. John sat down on the floor. Gosh! what hail! It rattled thunderously on the roof, battered at the sides of the car and bounced off the windows, while the Car Park was as white as if a snowstorm had blown over it! It was fun to be sitting snug inside here listening to it all. He wondered where Jim was, and hoped he had found as good a shelter. After about five minutes the hail stopped, but heavy rain continued to pour down. No use moving yet. John settled himself more comfortably and picking up a motoring map from the floor was soon so engrossed in 'Otwell and its Surroundings', in identifying One End Street, the Castle, Prison and other items of interest, that it was some moments before he realized the owners of the car had returned, were jumping in, breathless and wet, starting the engine and driving off!

'I'm *soaking*!' he heard the lady say, 'I've never seen such hail.' Her husband did not reply; he was speeding up in order to pass the traffic lights at the corner while the green beacon still glowed. By the time John had collected his wits, struggled to his feet, and summoned up courage to attract their attention, they were all far out on the London Road, 'doing', he saw by a glance at the speedometer, sixty miles an hour! Here indeed was an adventure – and entirely unsought.

*

Mr and Mrs Lawrence, the owners of the car, though certainly *surprised*, were not angry, as John was afraid they would be, when he explained what had happened.

'Of course you couldn't have stayed outside in that

hail,' said Mrs Lawrence sympathetically, 'it's still rain-
ing a little, will it be far for you to get home from
here?'

John looked about him. The car was drawn up at the
side of the road, there were fields and trees all round; it
must be some way from Otwell, but he had no idea
where. 'I'll manage all right,' he said shyly, and began
reluctantly to unfasten the door. What a fool he was!
Why hadn't he sat still longer and had a lovely drive
miles out into the country!

'Stop!' cried Mrs Lawrence suddenly, 'don't go, I've
just got an idea!' John held his breath. 'Henry,' she said,
turning to her husband, 'go on, we're late as it is, let's
take him back with us and he shall come to the party too
– Peter would love to have him!'

But Henry was more cautious. 'How'll we get him
home again – I want the car this evening,' he said.

''Bus,' replied his wife, 'there's one every two hours.
Would you like to come?' she asked turning to John.

Come? Where? Home-with-them-to-a-party-and-back-
by-bus-to-night! Coo!

'Quick!' said Mr Lawrence, his hand on the brake, 'is
it "yes" or "no"?'

'It's O.K.!' said John promptly, then remembering his
manners and Mrs Ruggles's intense dislike of this expression, he added, rather breathlessly, 'I mean, *yes, please!*'

As they went along, and during a picnic lunch at the
side of the road where John had his first drink of coffee
(tasted just like it smelled, he decided), Mrs Lawrence
explained why they were in such a hurry. They had been
away, visiting friends; today was their little boy's birthday, this afternoon there was to be a big party, and it
would never do to be late; that, she said, pointing to a
large box on the seat, was his birthday cake – coffee and

chocolate, mixed; it was to have nine candles – how old was John? Fancy, John was nine too! *and* he had a 'twin, *and* five other brothers and sisters. . . . By the time 'Home' was reached, John, who never suffered from shyness for long, had lost every trace of it, and the Lawrences certainly knew a great deal more about the laundry, scavenging and boot-repairing trades, and the ways of garages and filling stations, than they did when they got up that morning.

*

Coo! What a big house! Bigger'n Mrs Beaseley's up in Sycamore Road, bigger'n Otwell Priory where the Chief Constable lived, bigger'n the Majestic Cinema even, bigger'n . . . John's standards of comparison came to an end. And the rooms! One after another . . . and big, wide stairs – wider 'an the ones at school but all carpety instead of stone. It was amazing!

'This is the schoolroom,' said Mrs Lawrence opening a shiny white door, and instead of the rows of desks and maps John expected to see, he found himself looking into a brightly painted sunny room, without a trace of either. Instead, on a large table in the middle, stood a big bowl of goldfish, and in a little wooden cage with a glass top, what looked like, yes, really were, two live white mice! Round the walls were some rather untidy bookshelves, an ancient rocking-horse, and a cupboard whose doors were bulging open with such a thrilling assortment of toys that it was almost like looking at the Christmas Bazaar at Paul and Spotkeys in Otwell High Street!

In the midst of this splendour, at a small table in the window, hacking away at a bit of wood with a rather rusty knife, stood Peter, a boy about his own size, with dark hair, twinkling dark eyes, and a jersey even dirtier than John's own! After Mrs Lawrence had introduced them and gone away, they stood staring at each other in silence for a few minutes.

'He's smaller than me, but he's fatter,' thought John.

'He's bigger than me and wears a pale-blue jersey like a kid!' thought Peter.

But after John had been introduced to the goldfish and white mice, built a Meccano crane in less than five minutes (to Peter's admiration); ridden on the rocking-horse (to Peter's disgust – he had abandoned it at *least* two years ago!), conversation began to flow freely. In half an hour, Mrs Lawrence put her head round the door and suggested they might both be the better for a wash, and that Peter's guests would be arriving in about an hour.

Peter led the way to the bathroom. 'You wash first,' he said politely, turning on the taps.

But John stood rooted in the doorway. *What* a bathroom! All shiny white paint and glittery silver . . . reminded him of summat . . . yes . . . Otwell Hospital where he'd gone when he scalded his foot . . . but different . . . John sniffed . . . different *smell*! More like Mr Prestons-the-Chemists, he decided. And that bath! Why, one wouldn't mind having one twice a week in that – how different from their tub in the back kitchen at home with Lily Rose's and Kate's soapy water, and Jim and Jo yelling for their turns – and what was that funny thing above?

'That's a shower,' said Peter, following the direction of his guest's eyes. 'Like one?'

John had no idea what a shower was, except a shower of rain, but he was ready for anything. He nodded and grinned.

Peter grinned too. 'Take your jersey off,' he said. John obeyed, and now it was Peter's turn to stare. Why, the boy wore braces (*red* ones too!) *and* a belt – *staggering*! And of course to one who did not know that John's trousers were a late pair of Mr Ruggles's, and in spite of many alterations, required the most careful management, it *was*! Peter said nothing and turned the tap – unfortunately harder than he intended (he had meant to give John a sprinkle on his head) and now apparently, nothing would turn the water off!

Five minutes later, Mrs Lawrence coming in to see what all the giggling was about, found her guest soaked to the skin, and the bathroom an inch deep in water!

'I thought you got into our car to keep *out* of the wet!' she said.

'I *did*!' replied John, 'but it was a different *sort* of wet!'

Mrs Lawrence laughed, and Peter decided that even if he *did* wear a kid's jersey, and red-braces-and-a-belt, John was a boy after his own heart.

*

As they came down the stairs, half an hour later, clean and tidy, John wearing a white shirt and grey flannel suit of Peter's, Mr Lawrence met them.

'Look here, young man,' he said, 'I want your address; we can't keep you here all day without letting your parents know you're safe. I'm sending them a telegram.'

John's face fell. A telegram! If anybody in One End Street got a telegram, all the neighbours knew it at once, and usually what was inside it before evening; suppose some of the Gang heard of it, his lovely adventure would be no surprise at all!

'It's only to say you're all right,' said Mr Lawrence reassuringly. 'Listen, this is what I've said: "John perfectly safe; returning him tonight by seven o'clock bus".'

Oh, that wasn't so bad – nice and mysterious too.

How long would it take the telegram to get home? he asked. About an hour, Mr Lawrence thought. Coo! they'd all be at tea, except perhaps Jim. Wouldn't Lily Rose and Kate and Jo get a thrill! (He was not so sure about Mum and Dad.)

*

The guests were arriving, and John stood behind a tree feeling shy. They all seemed so fearfully clean and tidy and spoke rather like the gentleman whose voice was occasionally heard, wafting information about the weather and the price of hoggets, over their fence from Mr Hook-next-door's wireless. Everybody seemed to know everybody else, and John felt very out of the picture. Presently Mrs Lawrence discovered him behind his tree and introduced him so nicely to the arriving children, that instead of feeling just a boy who tried to mind cars and got stuck in one, he was made to feel quite an important person who had been doing the Lawrences a good turn, and got carried away in the process. Somehow Mrs Lawrence made it sound like that – and before John had time to feel shy again, there was tea!

He was hungry, for the picnic lunch had been light, and the thought of that chocolate and coffee cake (mixed), was stimulating to the appetite. There it sat, too large for any plate, on a silver plinth in the middle of the dining-room table, the sort of cake one dreamt of but never even saw, much less *ate*! It was covered with coffee coloured icing; little blobs of creamy chocolate sat all round the top; creamy chocolate lattice work covered the sides, and each of the pale-green candles stood erect in a sugar holder in the form of a flower. On the top was Peter's name and 'Many Happy Returns', in more creamy chocolate and little silver balls. John could hardly take his eyes from it to the other delicacies. He had never seen such a tea. The Otwell United Sunday Schools' Christmas treat paled beside it. There were no vulgar buns; the sandwiches – marvels of crustless refinement – were piled in pyramids, each pyramid topped with a flag announcing its variety; the bread and butter was thin as thin – cut cornerwise as Mrs Ruggles had it on very great occasions – while the cakes, their tops covered with aristocratic pale pink or green sugar, had

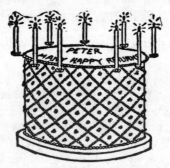

There it sat, too large for any plate, on a silver plinth in the middle of the table

a look of great breeding. Last, but not least, there were chocolate biscuits of the very best 'selected' brand – many three-decker varieties, and alluring shapes wrapped in coloured tin-foil. In fact, the whole tea had an air of having been recruited from the most exclusive tea shop.

No one spoke at first, but after one of the boys had upset a cup of tea over one of the girls' dresses, they brightened up and things became more lively. John's neighbour, a young lady of eleven who had so far not spoken at all, suddenly thrust a plate of tartlets under his nose. 'Do you like lemon-curd?' she demanded.

'Yes,' said John who liked almost anything.

'Not me,' said his neighbour. 'I ate some at a party last week, and was sick in the garden – it was awful!'

Awful! It must have been! John felt quite nervous; he had no idea how you got to the garden here. However, he took a tartlet, hoped for the best, and stared at the girl with round eyes.

'Do you go to school?' she asked next. John nodded. 'I'm in the third form,' she continued. 'Where are you?'

John looked puzzled. Forms were things one sat on. '*I'm* in a Standard,' he said.

'I thought that was a sort of flag,' said the girl, 'what does it mean?'

John found it hard to explain. 'There's seven,' he said, 'I'm in four. My sister's in seven – she's got a scholarship,' he added proudly.

'I've a cousin who's got one,' said the girl not to be outdone. 'She's going to Oxford, is your sister going to Oxford?'

'No,' said John, 'she's going to Otwell Central.'

'It sounds like a railway station,' said the girl, and after a pause, she added, 'you haven't handed *me* anything. *I* want a chocolate biscuit!'

John hastily passed the plate and when she had helped herself, although he hadn't *quite* finished his tartlet, took one too. This was evidently a mistake, for the boy on his other side glared at him fiercely, seized the plate and said coldly, '*after* you!'

His manner was not encouraging, but John thought he would venture on a little conversation. 'Do you go to school?' he asked presently, a little timidly.

'Of *course*,' replied the Fierce One, looking at him in amazement, 'don't *you*?'

'Yes,' said John.

'Where?' said the Fierce One.

'Park Road School, Otwell,' said John.

'Never heard of it!' said the Fierce One, and with a look of utter contempt he turned his back on John and began a conversation with the neighbour on his other side. John took refuge in another chocolate biscuit, and a few minutes later Mr Lawrence called out that if they'd all finished there were Surprises in the garden, and everybody flung aside their chairs and rushed outside.

The garden seemed about the size of Otwell Park but a great deal nicer, John decided. There were no notices about spitting or keeping off the grass or not picking the flowers; there were tennis courts, and on one of these the net had been taken down and the ground covered with rows of little flags. These were for the races, Peter explained, and in five minutes, the worries of polite conversation forgotten, John was hopping along between them in a sack race for 'under tens'. He came in third, rather disgusted with himself – he had been an easy first in the school sports last year – and determined to do better in the next event, an Egg and Spoon race. In keeping with the grandeur of the party, the spoons were silver, and the eggs real instead of the china variety. Fancy wasting all these eggs – what would Mum say! thought John; but how far more exciting than dropping a china one! Everyone competed in this race, and when he arrived first at the winning post with his egg intact, John felt very elated indeed.

'Please may I keep my egg?' he asked Mrs Lawrence. 'To take home to Mum,' he added.

'Of course!' she smiled, 'and we'll find some others to keep it company, but now you must get ready for the Treasure Hunt.'

A Treasure Hunt? How marvellous! John began to

quiver all over with excitement; would anyone in the Gang be able to relate an adventure to touch this!

Three things were hidden, and you could choose which you would look for. A tennis racket (that would take some hiding, thought John), a scout knife, and a camera, and Mr Lawrence was handing out little cards on which were printed clues for finding them.

John had no hesitation about his choice – hadn't he wanted a scout knife as long as he could remember – *for years and years*. He *must* find it! Four other competitors had apparently decided the same thing, and among them, as they all lined up, he was sorry to see the Fierce boy.

John studied his clue card intently. 'Take ten paces to the North West,' it began. That was easy, there was a weathercock on the house, and anyway you could watch the others. . . . 'Turn round three times, then run to the summer house and undo what you find there,' he read next.

'Ready?' called Mr Lawrence, blowing a whistle . . . 'One, two, three!' . . . They were off!

When he reached the summer house (a little dazed after the three turn-rounds, John saw four parcels (the Fierce One was busy with the fifth) lying on a table. All were exactly alike, wrapped up with brown paper and string and on each parcel was written: 'No KNOTS TO BE CUT,' *Oh*! those knots! John's fingers fumbled and fell over each other in their haste; the Fierce One was gaining, stripping off the paper, opening his parcel! At *last*! The final knot gave way and John tore off his paper. Inside was a box, and oh, how cruel! Inside it *another* box. and *more* knots! Inside this second box was a sealed envelope, and inside *that* (surely the last thing one expected to find) a piece of blotting-paper! Some writing had been blotted on it, and written on the bottom of the box, were the words, 'To read clue on blotting-paper, look behind summer house.' 'Must be a looking-glass,' said John to himself, for he knew of no other way you could read blotting-paper writing, and sure enough, hanging on a nail in the back of the summer house was a tiny mirror. 'Next clue will be found under the Fir Tree,' was all it revealed. Where *was* the Fir Tree? Right over the other side of the tennis court, apparently – the Fierce boy was speeding towards it! John set off at his fastest run. Why wouldn't one's legs go quicker – it was like a nightmare! A small boy thudded close behind him, then someone rushed past, and he caught a fleeting glimpse of the immensely long legs of the only girl competitor; what did *she* want with a scout knife, anyway, he thought indignantly!

Under the Fir Tree were buckets of water, and written on labels attached to their handles were the words, 'Carry me (without spilling) to the Tool Shed (N.E.); fill me with potatoes and return me here.'

Gosh! What was 'N.E.' – oh, *North East*, of course! The buckets were heavy although only half full, and the water splashed out a lot as one ran. It would be cheating to empty some out, John supposed. He struggled on and arrived just behind the long-legged girl. To his surprise Mrs Lawrence was sitting in the tool shed – how awful if one *had* cheated!

'I've spilt some!' he gasped.

'Never mind, tip out the rest, quickly,' she cried, and as soon as his bucket was empty she threw in a potato for encouragement. Very soon all five competitors were in the shed, falling over each other in their struggles to fill up their buckets. At last John's was full. The potatoes were heavier than the water had been, and it seemed an endless way back to the Fir Tree. Two buckets were already standing there by the time he reached it, and the Fierce One and the long-legged girl were rushing off again somewhere. John felt desperate. Where and what was the next clue!

'Look on the card,' whispered Peter who stood looking on.

John pulled it out of his pocket and looked. 'Last clue. Read carefully,' it said, and John read (carefully) :

> 'By the greenhouse you will see
> We once were six, we now are three;
> In the shed on their right,
> Sunny and bright,
> Marked with a ticket – that's Me!'

What *did* it mean! Anyway, it meant the greenhouse to begin with – lucky he'd noticed it beside the tool shed. . . . More running . . . he had hardly any breath left! He was glad to see the others were panting too, as a few minutes later all five of them stood gazing at the greenhouse, first from one side and then from the other. 'We once were six,' . . . what could it mean . . . who were 'we' to begin with! John began to feel quite ill with worry and excitement. Any moment one of the others might discover the meaning – *and* the knife! He had never thought so hard in his life – it was worse than a whole week's arithmetic problems!

The greenhouse was a three-sided affair. Leaning against one side was an old wooden bench; the door took up nearly the whole of another, while beside the third was a heap of mostly broken flower-pots, and some tubs of hydrangeas, also rather the worse for wear. For a moment John's attention was arrested by these plants. Mr Hook-next-door had two of them; they were the pride of his life; the whole of One End Street knew the story of how he had grown them from tiny cuttings given him by the head gardener at Otwell Priory; next year he hoped to have three! Almost without knowing it, John found himself counting these ... one, two, three. *Three*! 'We now are three'; he went closer. There, in the grass, if you looked *very* carefully, were three faint circular marks where *other* tubs had once stood! Three *and* three, six, 'we once were six!' He'd got it! ... 'In the shed on their right' ... which was their right – plants didn't have rights and lefts – anyway there was only one shed – the tool shed, where they'd got the potatoes, and John rushed towards it.

Mrs Lawrence was still sitting there, and smiled encouragingly. A second later, in dashed the Fierce One!

Things, things everywhere! Spades, rakes, hoes, flower-pots, sieves, water cans – enough to stock a shop – one didn't know where to begin to look, even! John paused, bewildered. He caught Mrs Lawrence's eye – she looked *very* amused. Why, he wondered suddenly, should she sit here, it seemed a funny place to choose – a very funny place! He looked at her more closely. On her knee she held a bright red hand-bag. It was slightly open. Peeping from it was something shiny – something 'shiny and bright Marked with a ticket'? Yes, a little white tag was hanging from it. .... John leapt towards it; the Fierce One leapt towards it (both at the same moment). There was a scuffle. The long-legged girl came running in and leapt on top of them both, and Mrs Lawrence and her hand-bag became, as she afterwards described it, 'Victims of a snatch and grab raid!'

*

John sat in the Otwell-bound bus. It was nearly nine o'clock and almost dark outside. Inside, the lights shone brightly, and there was a mixed smell of oil and petrol and hot stuffiness that made one feel very sleepy. On the seat beside him were several parcels; his still slightly damp clothes; a basket of eggs, a Meccano set (prize for the Egg and Spoon race) and a tin containing a huge piece of the birthday cake, chocolate biscuits and other delicacies for his brothers and sisters, while in a pocket of Peter's suit was a letter for Mrs Ruggles.

'Give this to your mother directly you get home and I'm quite sure she won't scold you,' had been Mrs Lawrence's last words as she said good-bye, and John was taking the very greatest care of it, patting his pocket at intervals to make sure it was still safely there. In his other pocket was the precious scout knife, and every now and then he would take it out, open the blades and other implements, gazing at them entranced, as if unable to believe so marvellous a thing were really his – it so very nearly hadn't been! ... one second later and it would now be travelling home with the Fierce One ... he had grabbed *just* too late! And John dwelt lovingly on his triumph for at least the twentieth time. It was a tale to make the Gang sit up all right! A tale to make every member green with envy – and it wouldn't be the only one he'd have to tell them! He began to go over the events of the day in his mind ... Slipping out quick before Mum could cop them – that had been an exciting moment ... then waiting in the Car Park ... getting inside the car ... looking up from the map and finding Mr Lawrence driving off ... dinner on the road (with coffee) ... Peter's house and the mice and building that crane so quick; the shower bath (here John smiled to himself) ... Mr Lawrence's telegram ... the *tea* ... the sports ... The Treasure Hunt ... why, there'd be enough adventures for a *dozen* meetings! ...

'Wake up, young man, wake up!' said a voice. John

opened his eyes; someone was shaking him. 'Wake up!'
Had it all been a dream then – was he no better than the
sort of boys in adventure stories who did marvellous
things and then, on the last page, the author would
calmly say they'd dreamt them all? . . . '*What a boy*!
Wake up do! – you're John Ruggles, aren't you – cove
here asking for you!' said the conductor, giving him
another shake.

John struggled to his feet, blinking at the bright light.
He fumbled in his pockets . . . yes, the knife was there . . .
and the letter . . . and the parcels were on the seat . . . it
was *real* all right! And there peering in at the door was
Mr Ruggles! 'Don't see him!' he was saying anxiously.

'Here I am, Dad!' cried John, collecting his parcels.
And although Mr Ruggles was expecting to see a pale-
blue jersey, there was no mistaking his son's red head as
it emerged from the bus, even though the pale-blue
jersey had been mysteriously exchanged for a neat grey
flannel suit!

*

'Well, I never did!' exclaimed Mr Ruggles as John,
putting all his parcels down on the pavement, insisted on
showing him the scout knife and all its glories and attempting to explain the day's excitements, almost in one
breath. 'Well, I never *did*!' he repeated several times on
the way home, and later, when they reached there, it
seemed Mrs Ruggles never did, either! For John, remembering Mrs Lawrence's instructions, before his
mother had had time to utter more than 'Why, whatever
clothes you got on!' had thrust the basket of eggs and the
precious letter into her hands, and taking advantage of
her surprise, skipped upstairs to see if Jim were still
awake – (if he was at home!). A few minutes later he

heard himself being called, and as soon as he entered the kitchen, he knew Mrs Lawrence had been right, there wasn't going to be no row, for there was Mum with her arm round Dad's neck looking as pleased as *pleased*! – whatever could it be, not just that basket of eggs surely! No! It required more than a basket of eggs to compensate

'*Well, I never did!*' *exclaimed Mr Ruggles*

Mrs Ruggles for her anxious day as Mrs Lawrence had evidently guessed.

Writing, as she explained 'from mother to mother', she had hoped Mrs Ruggles had not been too worried at John's disappearance, and then she had gone on to say how charmed she had been with him; his intelligence, his good manners, his thoughtfulness for his mother about the eggs – all signs of a most excellent upbringing. Both she and her husband would be delighted to meet Mr and Mrs Ruggles; as soon as the long days came

again they must come over and bring all the children
and spend a day in the country. She remained yours
sincerely, and p.s. would Mrs Ruggles please not trouble
to return the suit John was wearing, as it was getting a
little small for her son.

'Now that woman, dearie,' said Mrs Ruggles to her
husband when she finished reading the letter aloud, 'is
what I calls A Real Lady.'

Mr Ruggles replied there was no doubt about that,
and although it was late, filled his pipe again, and somehow, instead of being sent off to bed, John found himself sitting on the kitchen table recounting the day's adventures to his proud parents.

Half an hour later he was still there, while unseen,
round the half-open kitchen door, peeped his brothers
and sisters, listening with all their ears, their eyes nearly
popping out of their heads with envy and excitement!
And if Jo hadn't suddenly sneezed, he believed, he told
Jim next day, he'd have been sitting there till *Midnight*!
As it was, Mrs Ruggles shooed them all off to bed, only
remarking, quite mildly, as they'd all get their Deaths,
and such a thing must *never* happen again!

What *could* have been inside Mrs Lawrence's letter,
John wondered, as he fell asleep!

*

'I don't believe *half* of it!' said the Captain, Mr Henry
Oates, when the twins had finished relating their adventures at the lime kiln three days later. 'You've made
it up or got it out of a book!'

'What about this then!' cried Jim, jumping up very
pink in the face, and pointing to his forehead. Where the
bump had been was a glorious blue, green and yellow
bruise!

'*And* this!' and fumbling in his pocket he produced a crumpled ball of paper, which he carefully smoothed out and handed to the Captain. It was Mr Lawrence's telegram about John.

'And what about *this*!' shouted John, brandishing his scout knife in the air. There were shouts of laughter from all the members, someone called out 'Three cheers for the Red-Headed Ruggles', and in the din that followed, Mr Henry Oates, perhaps for the first time in his life, felt *very small indeed*!

Very quickly, however, he recovered his self-esteem. Had not he, against the judgement of the Gang, admitted these kids?

'What did I tell you?' he cried, when the uproar had died down. 'Didn't I say as twins always come out top!' And although some of the members privately doubted if they had heard this statement, Henry Oates was a big boy and strong; no one was bold enough to dispute it, and anyway, *twins certainly had*!

CHAPTER SIX

The Baby Show

'I CAN'T understand it!' said Mrs Ruggles to her friend Mrs Mullet, as they stood blocking the pavement outside the Home and Continental Stores with their respective prams during a lull in the family shopping one afternoon. 'Ten months old on Saturday and not a tooth showing! If it had been Kate now, what were the skinniest infant as ever you saw – mere rasher of wind she were – but a fine big baby like William! And if it isn't just our luck too! You see, Mrs Mullet, it's like this. Here's my husband been objecting all these years to Baby Shows –

both feet down you might say – and us with fine twins too! Obstinate? That's not the word; then one day, home he comes, full of this Feat what's holding in the old Priory Grounds next week. He says to me, "Rosie," he

*Blocking the pavement outside the Home and Continental Stores
with their respective prams*

says, "there's a Baby Show connected, what about our William?" "What about him?" I says, trying not to sound surprised, though you might have knocked me down with a feather! "William's finer nor any baby I've seen about," he goes on, "bigger'n Albert Bird's grand-

son now, wouldn't you say – they're showing *him*?" "Why,
Willliam 'ud make three of him, the miserable little
worm," I says – "bit slow with his teeth perhaps, but
he'll have plenty afore this show comes along." "It's
only six weeks," says Jo, "can't we do nothing to hurry
'em on – dog-biscuits or summat?" "Dog-biscuits!" I
cried, "why whatever are you thinking of, Jo Ruggles!"
Well, I thought it were only a father's anxiety for the
prize, Mrs Mullet, and I were so pleased at the idea of
showing a baby at last, and so afraid Jo might change
his mind, that I says no more. However, after a bit I began to get suspicious-like. Jo he keep on worriting about
William all day long; if it weren't his teeth it were his
weight or his hair or how long he could sit up. Then one
evening, coming back from the allotment we meets Albert Bird. "How's William?" he says. "Fine, thanks," I
replies. "Cut any teeth yet?" he asks. "Half a dozen any
day now," I says, and whatever's an old man like you so
interested for, I thinks to myself. "My George's baby's
got five," he says, and with that he slaps Jo on the back
and roars with laughter! Then I knew my suspicions
hadn't been for nothing; there *was* something up! "And
I'm not going home till I knows what!" I says. Well,
they was both hungry and wanted their suppers, so I
soon had it out of them. And would you believe it, Mrs
Mullet, it was *betting* they'd been – my Jo, what never
even backs a football, much less a horse, betting on a
baby! A whole half-crown on William against the baby
Bird! It gave me quite a turn; almost indecent it seemed,
but I've come round since; the deed's done, and better
babies than horses, I says to myself (though I hope it
won't lead to them), and after all I've always wanted to
show a baby, there's big money in prizes, *and* I wants
that half-crown back! But you see now what I mean, Mrs

Mullet, when I says luck's against us. Here's William, ten months old on Saturday, the show's next Wednesday, and not a tooth he's got!'

Mrs Mullet was very sympathetic. Although she was not certain whether she altogether 'held' with Baby Shows – anyway, her Muriel was nearly three and past the age limit – she understood the value of half a crown.

'You've tried the Welfare, I suppose?' she said.

Mrs Ruggles nodded. 'The doctor says "don't worry; his gums is hard as hard; he'll cut one any day," but she don't know *which* day no more than you or I, Mrs Mullet!' – Rusks? A wooden ring? A chicken bone to chew? Mrs Ruggles had tried them all.

'It will have to be the dog-biscuits,' laughed Mrs Mullet, as she prepared to move on.

'I'll not poison my William for all the Baby Shows in England!' declared Mrs Ruggles. 'It's Nature or Nothing for me; well, see you at the show, Mrs Mullet, and wish us luck!'

'That I will, Mrs Ruggles, you can count on me; I can't abide that George Bird family, anyway,' she added as they parted.

*

Wednesday dawned bright and sunny – a perfect day for a Feat, but it could not cheer the drooping spirits of the Ruggles family. William was toothless! He had been what Mrs Ruggles called 'fretty' half the night, a state that would have almost certainly heralded the arrival of a tooth in any of her other children. He now lay peacefully asleep on two cushions in a corner of the kitchen; his brothers and sisters crowded round him as if by looking they could in some way induce a tooth to show itself.

'Keep away from him, *do*,' said Mrs Ruggles sharply.
She had had a very disturbed night, and the prospect of
a day's ironing compressed into a hot morning was not
encouraging. 'No you *can't* all come to the Feat,' she
cried presently in answer to Lily Rose's inquiry. 'It'll be
sixpence each for your father and me, threepence for Peg,
and threepence each for all of you after five – that's half

His brothers and sisters crowded round

a crown. Lily Rose and Kate can come, the rest of you'll
have to stay at home.'

'Oh, let 'em all come,' said Mr Ruggles, getting up
from his breakfast and throwing half a crown on the
table. Mr Ruggles looked despondent; had he been allowed his way about the dog-biscuits, all, he was sure,
would now be well, but he knew it was more than his
life was worth to say so at the moment.

'Half-crowns seems nothing to you, these days!' said

his wife sarcastically, and Mr Ruggles put on his cap, hunched up his shoulders and departed to his work, looking what he felt, a very ill-used man.

No sooner had the elder children gone off to school, than William became 'fretty' again. Nothing seemed to soothe him. 'Wear himself out, he will, crying like this,' said Mrs Ruggles distractedly. To assist matters, Peg was more than usually full of spirits, and in her most adventurous mood, and by the time Mrs Ruggles had twice placed a knife and pair of scissors beyond reach, and rescued her daughter from the flour bin and blacklead box, she had decided she would support no Government in future that did not promise immediate erection of Nursery Schools to accommodate under-school-age offspring, and relieve harassed mothers.

But when she set forth at two o'clock, all these worries had vanished; Peg was subdued and tidy in a clean cotton frock, and William, in his best yellow woollies, was all gurgles and smiles again. Teeth or no teeth, thought Mrs Ruggles, he certainly was a remarkably fine baby, and she was much elated by some flattering remarks she heard 'passed' by the crowd outside the Manor gates, and the nervous glances cast at her perambulator by some of the other mothers.

The Fête, which was being held in the grounds of Otwell Priory, an old sixteenth-century house on the outskirts of the town, was in full swing when they arrived. Two marquees had been erected on the lawns, one reserved for tea, the other for the babies, while the less refined part of the entertainment, merry-go-rounds, Hooplas, coconut shies, etc., was relegated to a field behind the house. Even so, the noise they made was deafening, and Mrs Ruggles was concerned lest William, who had fallen asleep, should be awakened unnecessarily. There were numerous stalls dotted about, and still more numerous ladies who, with fixed smiles, approached Mrs Ruggles, begging her to guess the weight of a cake, name a doll, or forecast the number of fruits (species unknown) bottled in a jar. But Mrs Ruggles had not come to waste money; she had come to make it and retrieve her husband's half-crown, and she replied firmly 'not today, thank you,' and succeeded in reaching the baby-tent with her purse unopened.

Heavens! how many babies! Babies in every direction! Fat and thin, dark and fair, plain and beautiful, crying and placid! 'And they say the birthrate's going down!' said Mrs Ruggles to herself. 'Well, it don't look like it to me – not in Otwell, anyway.'

Each baby seemed to be accompanied by at least three adults, there was a fair sprinkling of small children, and the heat in the tent was stifling. William had awakened and was gazing about him in placid good humour; long might it last, thought Mrs Ruggles – but really, this heat! Phew!

Presently a bell was rung and a man's voice, speaking through a megaphone, demanded that everyone but the children's mothers please leave the tent, and as soon as a very large lady, who loudly and indignantly demanded whether aunties what had brought a motherless baby up from the month were to be excluded, had been reassured, the crowd of onlookers drifted away and the real business of the afternoon began. The babies were divided into two classes: those over six months but under a year old, and those of one year and over but under two years old. Two prizes were offered in each class, and a grand silver-gilt challenge cup for the best baby in the show.

'Look well on my dresser, that would,' thought Mrs

Ruggles, as she seated herself in the queue of waiting mothers and began to take stock of the other competitors. They seemed fine specimens on the whole, and she was sorry to see that the under one year section appeared to be by far the most popular. Farther up in the queue she spied young Mrs George Bird. Heavens! if that woman hadn't gone and dressed her poor child in bright pink woollies the colour of Otwell Rock . . . still, when you remembered what she could put on her own back, perhaps it wasn't so surprising . . .

At the end of the tent a space had been screened off by curtains, and presently the judges, a doctor, and two nurses in uniform, arrived to a mixed reception of cheering and wails, and disappeared behind them. Mrs Ruggles was pleased to see none of them were local people, and that the doctor was well on what she called 'the seamy side of forty', for she distrusted young men where babies were concerned. 'Shan't be long now!' said the fat auntie who had settled herself on Mrs Ruggles's left, and almost immediately the Voice, again speaking through the megaphone, announced that the judges were ready – would the competitors please come in one at a time; the results, the Voice added, would be announced outside the tea tent at five-fifteen.

*

It was over! Mrs Ruggles, William in her arms and Peg at her side, stood breathing fresh air (and sighs of relief) outside the tent. William had behaved perfectly, smiles and gurgles all the time, even when undressed and weighed, but whether he had won a prize – ! 'Ask me something else, Mrs Mullet!' said Mrs Ruggles to her friend who was waiting with her Muriel to hear how things had gone. 'That doctor was like a sphix, or whatever it is they calls them folks with no expressions. "Ten months?" he says to me. "Ten months Saturday," I says, and hands him the birth certificate. "No teeth through yet!" he says presently, "but will have any moment if I'm not mistaken!" and then he writes no end of things in a little book; try as I would, Mrs Mullet, I couldn't see *what*! "Let's have a look at that birth certificate again," he says, as I were going out, and a look at it he has, and hands it back without a word! No, you can't tell *what* they thinks, ever, Mrs Mullet, and the nurses – they're no better – something about a beautiful baby they says, and a seventh child lucky – just talk it is, they learns it them at the Hospital – it don't mean nothing. Well, there's nearly two hours to wait, Mrs Mullet, afore we knows the worst; how about a nice cup of tea?'

Mrs Mullet said it was just what she was thinking, and Peg Ruggles, who had been thirsty all the afternoon and said so, at frequent intervals, took Mrs Mullet's Muriel firmly by one hand, and Mrs Ruggles by the other, and steered straight for the tea tent!

*

It was after five o'clock, and a large and impatient crowd was collected in front of the tent. Everyone was full of excited speculation, for in a few minutes the names of the successful babies would be known.

Mrs Ruggles with William and Peg, and Mrs Mullet with her Muriel, stood in the front row and were joined at intervals by one after another of the little Ruggles, who had come from school and burrowed their way, impervious to rebukes, through the legs of the onlookers. Mr Ruggles and old Mr Bird had also arrived, much out of breath, and were panting somewhere at the back of the crowd. Everyone began to cheer when punctually at

five-fifteen the owner of the Voice, carrying his megaphone, arrived, mounted a chair and announced that, if
everyone was listening, he would now with much pleasure call out the names of the successful babies; the
prizes, he added, would be presented to the parents by
the Mayoress, inside the tent at five-thirty.

The cheering ceased, and a ripple of expectancy passed
over the crowd, and then in a silence that was almost

*The little Ruggles . . . burrowed their way, impervious to rebukes,
through the legs of the onlookers*

frightening, the Voice announced that the Grand Challenge Cup for the best baby in the show had been won by
Miss Ada Atkins, aged eighteen months, of Swanwell
village; the first prize for babies of one year and over, by
Master Freddie Fishwich, aged fourteen months, of Otwell; and the second prize in the same class by Miss
Hester (or Esther?) Stribbling, fifteen months, also of
Otwell; while in the class for babies under a year old, the
first prize was awarded to Master William Ruggles, and
the second to Master Albert Bird, both ten months and
both of Otwell! The crowd broke into loud cheers, and it
was some time before the Voice could be heard trying to
continue to speak above the din. 'I am asked,' it went on,

when at last there was a lull in the cheering, 'I am asked
to say, on behalf of the Committee, that while we are
delighted to welcome visitors from outside the Town, and
in no way grudge them our prizes, we think it is only fair
to let the inhabitants of Otwell know that the Grand
Challenge Cup has only narrowly missed being won by
the town; in fact, ladies and gentlemen, if the winner in
the under one year class, Master William Ruggles, had
only been a little hastier in the matter of cutting his
teeth, it certainly would have been, and when we have
all given three cheers for the winner, Miss Ada Atkins, of
Swanwell, I ask you to join in three cheers for Otwell's
Best Baby – Master William Ruggles. Now, all together,
three cheers for Miss Ada Atkins and her parents, hip,
hip –'

'Hurray!' yelled the crowd with great fervour, but
the cheers for 'Master William Ruggles and *his* parents'
were so deafening that you could hear the echoes almost
at One End Street!

'Will the parents please take their babies inside the
tent to receive their prizes,' said the Voice when at last
the applause died away.

'You take him, Jo, I can't!' said Mrs Ruggles, 'I'm all
of a tremble!' And Mr Ruggles, who was all of a tremble
himself, having pushed his way through the crowd to
the accompaniment of many hearty slaps on the back,
proudly held his son while Mrs Ruggles received a small
silver shield and an envelope containing a one-pound note,
with many congratulations from the smiling Mayoress.

'Let's get home, quick,' said Jo as they emerged from
the tent to be greeted by more cheering. Easier said than
done; everyone wished to see William, complete strangers wanted to kiss him, gentlemen of the press to take
his photograph. Poor Mrs Ruggles was surrounded,

unable to move in any direction, and it was only by the Voice calling through the megaphone that the winner in the raffle for the pair of embroidered bedspreads was being announced at the other end of the grounds, that the crowd could be induced to move away. William now began to cry dismally and his parents seized the opportunity for departure, joined the rest of their family, who in charge of Lily Rose were waiting with the perambulator near the gate, and made for home.

It was not the triumphal procession that one would have expected for Otwell's Best Baby! William's wails increased, and by the time One End Street was reached, he was screaming with a steady persistency that indicated a sleepless night for his relatives. 'Tired out he is, poor mite, and wanting his supper, he'll be all right as soon as he gets inside,' said his mother. But as soon as the front door was opened William redoubled his yells. 'Take him, Lily Rose,' commanded Mrs Ruggles, 'while I heats some milk.'

Lily Rose obeyed. 'Mum!' she cried excitedly a minute later, 'come, *come quick*! He's got it, it's come, *William's got a tooth*!' Mrs Ruggles flew to investigate. Too true! and now, alas, too late!

*

'Would have looked nice there, Jo, the cup,' said Mrs Ruggles sadly, as they passed the dresser on their way to bed that evening. 'Perhaps the dog-biscuits would have done it after all!'

But Mr Ruggles gallantly said no; his Rosie had been right; safer not to go agin' nature, and better William as he were, than a Cup on the dresser and William perhaps dying of dog-biscuits in a Hospital. 'Besides,' he added, 'we can always try again next year.'

Rosie looked at him sharply. 'We're not having no more babies,' she said firmly.

'I only meant,' replied Mr Ruggles, 'that as the age limit's two, William 'ud still be young enough next year.'

'I *believe*,' said Mrs Ruggles, looking hard at him, 'I *believe*, as you wants to make another bet!'

'I've made it!' said Mr Ruggles. 'Albert Bird's took me on again – five bob this time!' he added grinning.

But Mrs Ruggles's protests were drowned by renewed cries from William.

Another tooth was through!

CHAPTER SEVEN

Adventure in a Cinema

JO RUGGLES (junior) was a film-fan – that is to say, as far as Mickey Mouse was concerned – most other films bored him slightly, but for Mickey Mouse he would save up every halfpenny in order to take his place in the 'fourpennies' on Saturday afternoon. Fourpence took a lot of saving, for few pennies or even halfpennies came Jo's way. Lately he had taken to standing outside a large Tea Shop in the town holding open the door for customers in the hopes of earning some money. He looked so anxious and miserable that kind ladies often jumped to the conclusion he must be hungry and gave him pennies to buy cake and buns. It was becoming quite a profitable trade and sometimes Jo made as much as sixpence a week. Mrs Ruggles was unaware of this occupation, and would have been furious had she known of it. She had no idea that Jo spent most of his Saturday afternoons in the cinema, thinking he was playing happily in the Park with the other children. For Mrs Ruggles did not approve of cinemas, especially for the young. 'You're far better playing in the street or the Park,' was the invariable reply when approached for pennies for Mickey Mouse. 'Dirty stuffy places – full of germs and most of what they show unfit for children anyway.' Very occasionally – on birthdays and Bank Holidays – was she known to relent. Jo, however, had one grown-up friend who shared his enthusiasm and sometimes gave him halfpennies, and this was Mrs Hare next-door-but-one. She was a cleaner at the Majestic Cinema, the second largest in the Town, and, although his mother said she was a rotten one and no place but a cinema where it was mostly dark would employ her, to Jo she was a most romantic and thrilling person. She knew the coming programmes almost before the manager himself, and could tell one stories of all the stars, even of Mickey Mouse, and had a free pass for herself and her husband once a week.

Jo was consumed with jealousy of her husband, and

He would save up every halfpenny in order to take

would dream day-dreams of how, when he was grown up, he would murder Mr Hare, marry Mrs Hare, and share the free pass for life.

He used to scowl so heavily at Mr Hare when he met him in the street that that gentleman, not knowing what awful thoughts were passing in Jo's head, asked Mr Ruggles if that boy of his was 'all right' – 'his eyes you know,' he added hastily, seeing the startled expression on old Jo's face, 'seems to frown so as he almost squints sometimes!'

Mr Ruggles reported this to his wife, and she had some hard things to say of Mr Hare and the way some people were for ever criticizing and interfering with other people's children.

One Monday morning on his way to school Jo saw a coloured 'Silly Symphony' advertised for the coming Saturday. It was the first coloured one to be shown in Otwell, and Jo felt that he must see it if he died in the attempt. He had no pennies left, but he decided if he

his place in the 'fourpennies' on Saturday afternoon

went to the tea shop every evening till Saturday – that
would be five days – with luck he could make enough –
last week he had made fivepence and only been there
three times. But alas! he was twice kept in at school for
inattention (hardly surprising when his whole being was
centred on the coming film and the means of seeing it!)
and twice kept at home by his mother after he came back
from school 'minding' William – a task which, in common
with his brothers, he particularly detested, for William
was learning to crawl, and took a lot of minding. He also
had a good pair of lungs and knew how to use them if
his brothers got fed up, as they usually did, and smacked
or shook him. His yell would bring Mrs Ruggles to the
scene and then there would be trouble indeed for the
'Minder'. There were times when Jo hated William
nearly as much as Mr Hare, but not for long, for William
was his brother, and besides, when he was good and
gurgled and smiled it made Jo feel pleasantly grown-up
and superior whereas Mr Hare never made him feel anything but unpleasantly small and *inf*erior.

Friday morning came and Jo began to feel desperate,
for he had not *one* penny! He took great care to be extra
attentive at school for fear of being kept in again, and
very quiet through tea at home, hoping his mother would
not notice him, and he smiled happily when he heard her
tell one of the twins to 'mind' William. He was just going
to slip out of the door and rush off to the tea shop when
Mrs Ruggles caught sight of him, pushed a pair of Lily
Rose's shoes to be mended at-the-shop-round-the-corner
into one hand, and a parcel of laundry to be delivered in
the next street into the other.

It was certainly not Jo's lucky day. He handed in the
shoes and then ran as fast as he could with the laundry,
tripped over a stone and fell, cutting his knee badly and

tearing a large hole in the parcel. For a wonder he had a handkerchief, which he used alternately on his eyes and his cut knee, finally tying it round the latter. He deli-

'Minding' William

vered the battered parcel successfully, and then made for the tea shop. But he had wasted quite ten minutes, and his cut knee caused him to limp slightly and delayed progress still more, and to his horror as he passed the Town Hall clock, he saw it was after half past five – and the shop shut at six. Earn fourpence in half an hour – never! Why, oh why, he thought, hadn't he kept the remains of last week's pennies instead of buying Liquorice All-Sorts – the very thought of them made him feel sick now. Well, it was too late to think of that!

He reached the shop and took up his stand outside the door hoping there would be plenty of customers. There were not, and only one lady took any notice of him at all.

'Hullo,' she said, and then looking more closely, 'Why, it's Jo Ruggles! What are you doing here, Jo?' she asked kindly, wondering from his dirty face (he was covered with mud from his fall), and general untidy appearance and the fact that he seemed to be begging at the door, if his father was out of work. 'Mum and Dad all right?'

'Fine, thanks, Miss,' said Jo, and blushed scarlet. Horrors! it was Miss Clements, a teacher from his school, not in the Infant Department to which he still belonged, but she taught his brothers, and knew him well by sight. Suppose she told his Mum he was here – or even the twins!

'Hungry?' inquired the lady.

Jo nodded. He wasn't particularly, but he hoped it might mean a penny.

'Come inside,' she said, 'and I'll buy you a bun.'

Oh dear, that was very nice, but Jo wanted a penny – four pennies – more than all the buns in the shop! But it was no good. Two buns, one currant and one covered with white sugar were bought and presented to Jo, and the kind lady said 'Good-bye, see you at school on Monday,' and went off wondering if Mrs Ruggles really *could* afford to feed all those children properly, and if she ought to see the Head Teacher about their getting a free meal at school.

Jo looked sadly at the buns. The shop was closing and there would be no more customers. He stood for some time on the pavement outside, a bun in either hand, considering the situation. Then, quite suddenly he had an idea, a big *thrilling* idea – so thrilling that he almost dropped the buns! How *stupid* he was not to have thought

He stood . . . a bun in either hand, considering the situation

of it before! He put a bun very carefully into each pocket and ran quickly home.

His brother John was sitting just inside the door holding one end of a skipping rope to the other end of which was attached William. William was uttering strange bleats – prelude to one of his famous yells. John looked depressed, but brightened up as he saw Jo. 'Here, mind him a bit, Jo,' he said. 'I've promised Arthur Muggins to meet him at six, and it's nearly half past now.' Jo agreed readily enough. He did not care how long he 'minded'

William this evening. He took hold of the skipping rope and sat down. William looked offended at this change of minders, and immediately opened his mouth wide to let out a good roar. But Jo was resourceful. Licking his finger he rubbed it on the sugar bun in his pocket and popped it into William's mouth. The baby became quiet as if by magic!

'Funny,' said John, 'I never knew giving him a finger to suck would stop him yelling – I'll remember that next time,' and he rushed off. Jo smiled to himself. He felt superior and altogether mysterious and important.

*

Next morning being Saturday, Jo was free to do as he wished, provided he could escape William and all errands. Directly he had swallowed his breakfast he was out of the door like a streak of lightning. He stopped for a moment at the corner of One End Street and looked cautiously round. No one calling him; no one in sight except a whistling errand boy and women shaking mats at their doors. He was free! His adventure had begun!

Jo ran straight to the Majestic Cinema. There was Mrs Hare next-door-but-one on her hands and knees, scrubbing the grand marble steps (the Majestic Cinema was a cross between a Rajah's palace and a Town Hall).

'Morning, Jo Ruggles,' called Mrs Hare, 'you're out early – going to see the coloured film this afternoon?'

Jo shook his head.

'No pennies? – oh, well, there'll be another soon,' said Mrs Hare consolingly; 'week after next I think I heard that young chap in the box office say.'

Week after next! Jo gasped – it was Eternity. Why, he could hardly wait till this afternoon! *Week after next* – he might be **dead** by then – would be for certain if he had to wait all that time! How lucky, how *very* lucky he had had such a wonderful Idea!

However, now that the moment for carrying it out had

He stopped . . . at the corner of One End Street and looked cautiously round

come, he felt rather alarmed. He stood watching Mrs Hare.

Presently the steps were done, and she began to clean the brass on the ticket office. The big doors of the cinema stood open. Jo peeped in. How strange it all looked! A sort of twilight reigned, and the rows and rows of tipped-up seats looked sad and forlorn. Jo felt a little frightened and *very* small. He looked back at Mrs Hare. She was busy at her brass and singing cheerfully to herself as she polished; she had forgotten him.

Jo slipped inside. It was difficult to see at first, but his eyes soon became accustomed to the half light. He looked carefully round. No one about. Then he ran quickly down the centre gangway and crept under the curtain that screened the orchestra from the audience.

The Majestic Cinema was a little behind the times in its music and still employed 'real' musicians instead of the modern 'canned' variety. There was accommodation for three of these gentlemen behind the green curtains, and it was here that Jo meant to carry out his great Idea, which was to hide until the cinema opened in the afternoon, when he would creep out and take a seat in the front row! He looked round him. The thing now was *where* to hide, for there seemed little to hide *in*! There was a piano, two music stands, three chairs, half a dozen palms in pots and an untidy heap of old music. Jo was small, but not small enough to be concealed by any of these things except the piano. He looked behind it. Ah, that was better, there was a large wooden packing-case and what looked like an old table cloth thrown over it. Jo lifted the cloth. The box was empty except for a few sheets of music. He climbed inside and sat down. It made a nice little house, and there was plenty of room even if he were to lie down; but it was hard. Perhaps it would be better if he wrapped the old cloth round him! He did so as best he could and lay down. Very comfy! Would it be long to the afternoon performance, he wondered. He crawled out and looked at the clock. Half past nine – and the performance began at two. Jo counted on his fingers

– four whole hours and a half to wait – impossible! He
climbed back into the box and considered. It was very
quiet. After what seemed like two hours at least, the
clock struck ten. Jo decided he was very hungry; his
breakfast had been hurried and obviously today he
would get no dinner. Well, he would have his dinner
now. He drew from his pockets the two buns he had been
given yesterday. (He prided himself on the care with
which he had concealed them from his family.) The sugar
one was in rather a melty state and covered with hairs
and fluff; however, it tasted all right. The other was of
the currant variety and had survived better. He ate them
very slowly, spinning out the meal as long as possible.
When they were finished he felt more cheerful. He looked
at the clock again – only ten past ten! Perhaps if he could
pretend it was night and go to sleep, the time would not
seem so long. Mrs Hare or someone had shut the door
now, and he could no longer hear the faint sound of
the traffic from the street – nothing but the ticking
of the clock. It was monotonous and soothing. '*Mic*-
key Mouse,' it seemed to say, '*Two* o'clock, *Mic*-key
Mouse' . . .

In less than ten minutes Jo was fast asleep.

*

He was awakened some hours later by a bright light
and the sound of voices. The orchestra had arrived.

Jo sat up in his box and saw three men staring down at
him; he was very, very frightened. This was not at all
what he had intended. He had meant to crawl out before
they came and sit in the front row. *Now* what would
happen? Probably the manager, or worse still, a policeman would be called and he would be told never to set
foot in the cinema again, *and* he would not see the coloured

film! Two big tears rolled down Jo's cheeks. He looked timidly up at the men.

'Cheer up, Sonny,' said one, a big fat man who played the 'cello, 'and tell us how you got in that box on top of my music.'

'We're not going to eat you,' said another, the little man who played the piano, as Jo made no answer.

The third, the violinist, said nothing, but he looked at Jo kindly in a considering sort of way; he too, had had an idea. 'I think,' he said at last, 'he came to see the film, isn't that it, young man?' Jo sniffed and stood up. 'Well,' said the violinist, and he smiled, 'you don't answer my question.'

Jo caught the smile, and in spite of his damp eyes and sniffy nose, smiled back. He nodded.

'I thought so,' said the violinist. 'and what time did you get into the box, may I ask?'

'Half past nine,' said Jo, hanging his head.

'Good Heavens!' exclaimed the fat man.

'And no dinner, I suppose!' continued the violinist.

'Buns,' said Jo. 'Two,' he added, determined to make a good show of it.

The men looked at each other.

'What do they do with bad boys who try to get into cinemas without tickets?' said the fat man to the other two.

'I rather think,' said the violinist seriously, 'they get up a *Collection* for them!'

Jo's smile faded. He stared, horrified. 'A Collection' – did that mean someone, a policeman perhaps, would call and collect him like the man called to collect the rent, and perhaps take him away to the Police Station, or worse still, the Prison outside the town?

'Please, *please* don't collect me,' he cried, jumping out

of the box. 'I'll go home, truly, I will. I'll never try and get in for nothing again, only please, please don't let me be collected.'

The men all laughed. 'We don't want to collect you,' said the violinist, 'we've got boys enough of our own; we want to get rid of you and collect our music and begin playing. Here you are, here's sixpence; run along to the office and get a ticket and say I sent you, and mind, don't you ever do this again,' he added, looking very fierce, 'or next time a policeman or someone really *will* collect you,' and he picked Jo up and lifted him over the orchestra railings.

*

'Where have you been?' asked his mother when Jo got home well after tea time, having sat till the last note of 'God Save the King' – and after.

'Gentleman give me sixpence to see Mickey Mouse,' he answered, blushing to the roots of his hair.

'Did you ask him for it?' said Rosie sharply.

'No,' said Jo, 'he just give it me.'

'Then you must have been hanging about outside the cinema instead of playing in the Park with the others. I won't *have* it, I tell you, and where were you dinner-time?'

Fortunately, just at this moment the twins, who were having a wrestling match in a corner of the kitchen, fell over on top of William, and in the uproar that followed, the scolding of the twins and the kissing of William, Jo's adventures were forgotten by everyone but himself. He lovingly turned two pennies over and over in his pocket – two pennies towards the next 'Mickey Mouse' ('week after next') – no Liquorice All-Sorts this time!

CHAPTER EIGHT

What Mr Ruggles Found

IN spite of a wife and seven children (not to speak of Ideas) Mr Ruggles was a very contented sort of man. When the wind was in the East and blew bits of dirt from his dustbins and cart into his eyes and mouth he spat and swore a bit, but it was soon over. So long as he had his job and his family were well and happy, and he could smoke his pipe and work in his garden, see his mates at the Working Men's Club once or twice a week, dream about his Pig, and have a good Blow Out on Bank Holidays, he wanted nothing more. Mr Ruggles always 'went a bust' as he expressed it, on Bank Holidays. For the August one he would do any odd job he could get, and take the whole family for a day to the sea six miles away. They would start off about eight o'clock, by the first bus, each member of the family carrying something, one a thermos, another a loaf or a bag of buns, and Mrs Ruggles bringing up the rear with the last baby in a folding push-pram. If it was fine they would have a great day! First a walk along the promenade, then Dinner on the beach about twelve – all the Ruggles sitting in a row *gorging* pork-pies and doughnuts and bananas, while the sea-gulls flew expectantly round.

After dinner they would go on the Pier and put pennies in all the automatic machines, and watch games of Football, Cricket and Boxing, or thrillers like the 'Burning House', in which the firemen rescued a lady in her nightdress from the top bedroom, or, best of all, 'The Execution', a drama in three acts – 'The Condemned Cell', 'The Walk to the Scaffold', and 'The Hanging'. This last was so popular that Mr Ruggles often wasted as much as threepence on it, although Rosie said it was 'highly unsuitable' for children. After the Pier they usually paddled and Mrs Ruggles enjoyed this more than anyone.

'I has my hands in water every day,' she would say, 'and now I'm going to give my feet a turn!'

In the afternoon there were the Pierrots or the Band, or, if you were careful and knew your way about, and

All the Ruggles sitting in a row gorging . . . while the sea-gulls flew expectantly round

secured chairs in the right spot, both at once – Pierrots to the right, Band to the left – confusing at times, but none the less enjoyable, especially when you knew you were getting both free.

After this there was Tea. Tea was a great feature of the day, and the Ruggles would usually join with some of their friends and patronize one of the numerous shanties on the Front. There were dozens of these, and every kind of tea was advertised. 'High Tea', 'Devonshire Tea', 'Plain Tea', 'Fish Tea', or 'Fish *and* Chips tea', in fact, the choice was overwhelming! But the Ruggles were experienced! They looked carefully inside before entering, and if they saw a notice to the effect that 'tea and minerals will not be served to those bringing their own food', they moved on, for they always brought their own bread and butter and tea too sometimes, for these, though necessary, cost money, and they preferred to spend that on shrimps and cockles and other delicacies when at the seaside.

Most of the 'shanties' had names such as 'Home Sweet Home', 'The Nut-Shell', 'The Old Firm', or 'Where the Kettle Sings', but the Ruggles favourite bore the legend, 'Tea as Mother Makes it'. Here you were allowed your own bread and butter, and 'Mother', a lady of gigantic proportions, gave you, Mr Ruggles declared, more shrimps to the pint than any other establishment in the town.

Even a wet Bank Holiday was enjoyable at Brightwell, for the day could be spent under cover in the Amusement Arcade with sometimes a finish up at the Cinema.

Other Bank Holidays were not so luxurious. Boxing Day they usually all went to the Pantomime and at Whitsun and Easter, if funds were good, sometimes Mr Ruggles would hire a broken-down Ford and they would have a-Day-In-The-Country, but lately Rosie had complained she found this Dull.

Mr Ruggles's great ambition was to take the whole family to London one Whitsun Bank Holiday, for the great Cart-Horse Parade in Regent's Park. His brother Charlie, who was in the same line of business, had often written and asked him to come and bring them – his dust-cart had won many prizes in the show in which all the London heavy dray and cart-horses compete, and he wrote what a fine sight it was and how Jo and Rosie would enjoy it; there was room for twenty at least in his cart, and the children would have the time of their lives.

But alas! Mr Ruggles had never yet succeeded in saving enough money, even with odd jobs, for the fares to London.

Though all the children went half price, the younger ones with luck 'in arms', it cost too much. Every year his brother wrote asking them, and every year Jo had to write back he was afraid not, not this year; perhaps next.

At last Charlie wrote and said if he won first prize again this year – and he had every hope of doing so – he would send his brother something towards the fares. Unfortunately he had bad luck, his horse sprained its leg two days before the show, and Charlie only got a second prize in consequence. All hope for next Whitsun faded away again, and Mr Ruggles, as usual when in financial difficulties, fell back once more on the Pig Question. If he bought one at once and fattened it up, he mused, he could sell it nicely by next Whitsun and they could all go to London. He was very happy thinking about this for several days and at last broached the subject to his wife.

'Really, Jo Ruggles,' she cried, 'do have some sense. It's not money you'll *make* over a pig but money you'll *lose*.'

'How's that?' said Jo, 'we've enough to feed it, and if we haven't, Hook next door will be glad to give me his scraps – he's often said so.'

'I dare say,' replied Rosie, 'and how long do you think it will be before that Nosey-Parker of a woman, Mrs Smith-down-the-road, will have the Sanitary Inspector after you – I've told you before – every time you mention that Pig – two days I give her and then you'll be lucky if you get off with a Caution.'

'It would be a first offence, anyway,' murmured Jo.

'Well, I'm taking no risks,' replied Rosie. 'If you want a Pig, you get a bigger allotment and put it there.'

Mr Ruggles sighed. Renting a bigger allotment cost

money, and buying a pig cost money, and by the time he'd done both he'd be no nearer the fares for the trip to London even if he sold the Pig well, and if he *didn't* sell the Pig, where'd he be – In Debt. (And this was where Mr Ruggles had never been yet except for one awful winter when he'd hurt his leg and the Insurance money about paid for the rent and coal.)

'Well, I dare say I'll get an Idea for making the money one day,' he said to himself, 'or something will turn up.'

Something *did* 'turn up' – sooner than Mr Ruggles expected, and in the most *un*-expected way!

*

Less than a week after the conversation about the Pig, Jo was going his round one morning, emptying dustbins with his mate Mr Bird. They usually took it in turns for one to hold the horse while the other brought out the rubbish – not that the horse – ancient grey which looked as if it only needed a stand and four wheels to qualify for any nursery, *needed* holding, but more for the look of the thing and as a rest from carrying the dustbins which were heavy and tiring.

It was Mr Ruggles's turn to empty. He knocked at the side gate of No. 9 Wistaria Avenue which was always kept locked – for no reason which he could see, except that the owner was peculiar in his ways – an author by trade and apparently suspicious of everyone who came to the house. The same thing happened every Tuesday. After five or six of Mr Ruggles's knocks, the gentleman would appear at a top window (still in his pyjamas, although it was past eleven o'clock) throw out a key and say briefly, 'Call when you've finished.' Mr Ruggles would do so, throw up the key which the author caught deftly, slamming down the window with a surly 'thanks'.

It was a quick job, No. 9, the dustbins were always light, crammed full of old tins and bits of paper. No 'pickings' ever to be had here! At some houses they did quite well – old pairs of shoes, bits of carpet, bead-necklaces, a leaking saucepan, which only needed a little soldering, foreign stamps on old letters (which Mr Bird collected for his son), picture papers, many empty bottles and once a full one, a large unopened bottle of beer which had been

Crammed full of old tins and bits of paper

thrown out by mistake! 'A very bad sign,' Mr Bird had said, and why it wasn't broken Jo couldn't imagine! How they had enjoyed that beer, sitting side by side on the Dust Dump outside the Town drinking alternately out of the bottle! After this Mr Bird always had hopes of finding some treasure among the rubbish. 'A Diamond Tiara – £500 reward, and we'd retire for life, mate,' he would say, but Mr Ruggles was less optimistic; he had been longer at the job than Mr Bird, and so far the beer had been his best find. But one never knew.

'Easy life, that,' he remarked to Mr Bird as he came out of No. 9. 'Just writing, and sleeping till after eleven!'

'No money in it, Ruggles,' replied Mr Bird, 'no money; too many books about nowadays – why think of the hundreds in the Public Library in this Town alone – not to mention the shops. And look at the tins in his dustbin – enough for a family of ten! You take my word for it, Ruggles, when a single man gets down to *tins* like that, he's not prospering. 'Igh 'opes and 'errings, that's what his trade is – and *tinned* 'errings at that,' he added.

They finished Wistaria Avenue which was the last road on their round, and made for the Dust Dump outside the Town. It was a hot day for the time of year, and by the time they reached the Dump Mr Bird was reminded of the bottle of beer they had found.

'Never another find like that, Jo,' he said.

''Fraid not,' replied Mr Ruggles as he began to let down the back of the cart in order to tip out the rubbish. They always emptied it into a heap and then raked through it with old shovels for 'luck'; later it had to be neatly flattened out, for the Town Council proposed building a Park on this welter of tins and bits in the far distant future. 'Laying the foundation stones,' Mr Bird called it.

They raked and shovelled in silence for some time, and then Mr Ruggles called out 'Stamps for you, Bird,' and bent down to pick up an envelope. Mr Bird straightened himself up. 'Chuck it over, mate,' he said briefly. 'If we can't have beer, we may as well have stamps.' But Mr Ruggles did not 'chuck it over'. Instead he stood up and began examining the envelope; it was bulky; sticking out of it was a £5 *note*! He pulled the note out and held it to the light as if unable to believe his eyes.

'What is it, Ruggles, found a fiver?' inquired Mr Bird sarcastically.

'Yes, I have,' replied Jo unexpectedly. 'Six of them,'

he added calmly, peering into the envelope, 'and one, two, three, four, five, six, seven, eight, nine, ten, *eleven* £1 notes too!'

Mr Bird dropped his shovel and came over to where Mr Ruggles was standing. 'You're joking,' he said. 'They're never *genuine*.'

'Well, they looks all right to me,' said Jo, 'but maybe you're right; more than likely they're a fake – a find like that's too good to be true.'

'They *looks* all right, certainly,' said Mr Bird, regarding the notes as if they were a bomb and might explode at any moment. 'Just think of you finding this lot all along of looking at an old stamp, and me only just saying as that beer were our first and last find!'

'And you asking me if I'd found a fiver!' chuckled Mr Ruggles – 'why, there's £41 here! But it's no good,' he added sadly, after a moment's reflection, 'we can't keep it; some fool what's richer than he deserves to be will be making a song about these – you'll see. It's the Police, Bird, all right.'

Mr Bird scratched his head. 'Well it do seem a blinkin' shame to think you've found all that and got to hand it over – could you keep one or two of the one pound notes, do you think?'

'I don't see as I could,' replied Mr Ruggles, 'it ain't right to start with, and if it were, the bloke whose money it is would soon miss them when the rest were given back; pretty rotten luck it is though,' he added sadly – 'set us both up nicely, wouldn't it,' and he sighed as he thought of the Pig and the Cart Horse Parade and the Price-of-Tickets-to-London; here, right in his hand, was the price of two hundred tickets!

'Why, you'd never meant to *share* it, Ruggles?' said Mr Bird, astounded.

'Why, of course, Bird,' replied Jo, 'we've always shared out "pickings", haven't we?'

'Well, yes, we have,' assented Mr Bird, 'but this seems different somehow.'

'It's a safe offer anyway,' said Mr Ruggles, 'because there'll be nothing to share unless they give us a reward and I've no great hopes of that – price of a glass of beer is about all we'll get if we get anything; only the other day I read in my paper about a chap what found a pearl necklace in his taxi – worth thousands it was. Five shillings reward he got, and when someone said it was a shame giving him so little, the lady as the pearls belonged to said nowadays people was so well-educated by the State they'd no excuse *not* to give back things they found – knew quite well what they was worth, and the man was only doing his duty! Perfect lady she was. Don't you count on no rewards, Bird!'

'I won't,' said Mr Bird, 'but I can't help *hoping*. Wonder who the fool was as chucked those notes away. "Short, 9 Wistaria Avenue",' he read on the envelope. "Short" – good that – short he is for the present and deserves to be. "Nine Wistaria Avenue" – Jo Ruggles, I'll eat my hat if it ain't that author with all the tins – isn't he 9?'

'That's right,' said Mr Ruggles, 'and it just shows, Fred Bird, as empty tins *don't* always mean empty pockets!'

*

Mr Ruggles came home late to his dinner. He looked depressed. His wife was in a particularly good temper, for the matron at the Welfare Centre had told her that morning that Peg and William did her credit, yes indeed they *did*.

'What's up, dearie?' she said to Mr Ruggles, as he came in – 'you looks upset – and you're very late. I've kept your dinner hot, and a good one it is too; steak-and-kidney, jam roll, and a bit of that cheese you like, that's ready to walk off the table.'

Mr Ruggles sat down. 'It's took me appetite away,' he said.

'What has – the smell of the cheese?' asked Rosie.

'I'm fair upset,' continued Mr Ruggles. 'It's no wonder to me some chaps turn Communist; no wonder at all.'

'What *are* you talking about?' demanded Mrs Ruggles. 'Who or what's took your appetite away – another Dead Cat?' (For sometimes Mr Ruggles encountered one of these or, what he disliked still more, Drowned Kittens, in his dustbins.)

'Rosie,' he said, solemnly but impressively, 'I've come from the "Station"!'

'You sound as if you'd come from a funeral – what was it – a street accident?' then, as Jo made no reply – 'Jo, not anyone we know been done in, I hope?'

'No, Rosie, it wasn't that sort of accident,' replied Mr Ruggles.

'Well, whatever it was, for goodness sake get it out soon or your dinner'll be stone cold.'

At this suggestion Mr Ruggles finally 'got it out', and told the story of his morning's adventures.

Rosie listened with breathless attention, her head slightly on one side, her hands firmly planted on her hips. The children, already late for afternoon school, stood or sat about with wide eyes and gaping mouths.

'Get off to school,' said Rosie, turning round for a moment, as Mr Ruggles paused for breath. Not one moved, but Mrs Ruggles was too absorbed in her husband's story to notice.

'We got to the "Station",' said Mr Ruggles,' and asked to see the cop in charge of the Lost Property Department. Who do you think it was? Why, old John Simmons – you remember him, Rosie – sat next us at the Panto with his wife and kids last Christmas Bank Holiday?'

Rosie nodded. 'Go on,' she said briefly.

'Well,' continued Mr Ruggles, 'we told him what we'd found, and who we thought it belonged to, and he said it would be dealt with at the proper quarter, "and I hope you both gets a good reward, straight I do," he says, "but don't count on it; times aren't what they were"; and then,' said Mr Ruggles simply, 'we came away. But it's knocked me out, Rosie,' he added, 'finding all that money and not being able to touch it and us wanting those train fares so badly, to say nothing of the Pig.'

Mrs Ruggles was very sympathetic.

'Slip out and fetch your father a pint of beer,' she said to Lily Rose, 'and get off to school the rest of you – *quick now*!'

Lily Rose took the jug and went out, the others lingered.

'Couldn't you have kept just *one* pound, Dad?' asked Kate.

'Will you *go*,' cried Rosie, 'can't you see we're worried!'

The little Ruggles looked wise. 'Worried' in their experience was another name for what in a child was called 'in a shocking temper'. They scuttled off like rabbits.

'Have your dinner now, dearie,' said Mrs Ruggles.

*

For three days Mr Ruggles heard nothing more of his 'find', and the whole family lived in a state of suspense; would Dad get a reward – would it be 'only the price of a glass of beer', or would they all be able to go to London; or would it, as Kate mournfully suggested, 'be just enough to take Mum and Dad and none of us,' or, worse than anything, would there be no reward at all!

Meanwhile at No. 9 Wistaria Avenue, Mr Short, the author, having retrieved his lost property from the Police Station, sat in his study smoking cigarette after cigarette, and what he called 'Pondering a Problem'. He had spent an anxious two days – the loss of the notes had been a Problem all right, and he had been very thankful indeed to get them back, for they were not his own, but sent by an old sailor friend, who had been saving them for years, to be invested. *How* they had got in the dustbins was a mystery – must have mixed them up with that Swedish correspondence that came the same day he supposed – careless idiot that he was. Well, thank Heaven, they were now safely in the post to London! The Problem now was the problem of a reward to the Dustman who had found them, and Mr Short sighed deeply as he pondered. Such honesty, he felt, should be rewarded on the spot, and he would have liked to call on this Mr Ruggles or whatever his name was, straightaway, there and then, press a £5 note into his hand, and assure him of friendship for life! As it was . . . and he sighed again. Should he go and call on this man, tell him the truth – try and convince a working man with a wife and (was it ten children the police-sergeant had said?) that he, a single gentleman, renting a house in Wistaria Avenue, was not only 'hard up' but *broke* – the possessor of ten shillings, and a letter from the Bank stating that his overdraft had reached its limit? Useless, he felt; on the other hand, he hated the idea of so honest a creature as this Mr Ruggles appeared to be, left thinking he was to receive no recognition of his good deed and probably by this time wishing he'd never returned the notes at all. No, there was only one thing to do, he decided; write a letter, offer his thanks and explain, that, owing to pressure of work, he was unable to call at present, but hoped to do so next week. (By then, if not before, he would be in funds again, and though £5 would still be beyond him, he would have *something* to press into Mr Ruggles's hand.) He took up a pen and scribbled a note. When it was done he sighed again, but this time with relief. He had pondered to some purpose at last. Now for a cigarette, the newspaper and peace! He sat down, but a second later jumped up, threw down the newspaper, glanced at the clock, muttered something under his breath, and, seizing a hat, hurried out of the house in the direction of the High Street, lighting a cigarette as he went!

*

The same evening about five o'clock there was a knock at the door of No. 1 One End Street, Mrs Ruggles opened it, and standing on the steps was a spry little man with what looked like a leather box slung over his shoulder.

'Mrs Ruggles?' he inquired, and without waiting for a reply, handed her a card on which was printed, 'Mr Walter Wilkins, Journalist.' 'I'm from the *Otwell Gazette*,' he continued, taking off his hat and making Rosie a wonderful bow. 'Been hearing very interesting news about your husband, Mrs Ruggles – Mr Short the author called at our office this morning – thought we'd like the story for our issue tomorrow, *and* we should, Mrs Ruggles, *and* we should! Mr Ruggles not in yet, I suppose?' he went on, stepping past the astonished Rosie into the kitchen and glancing round.

'No,' she replied, feeling rather annoyed, 'be back any minute now though.' (What a cheek – walking in like that! Well, anyway, Jo's bloke, Mr Short, were still alive – must have got his notes all right – pity *he* didn't call!)

'Dear me, what a very large family,' cried Mr Wilkins, as child after child emerged from behind drying sheets and table cloths, and stared at him. 'Six, seven, eight – how many is it?'

'Seven,' said Rosie, proudly.

'"We are seven," ha, ha! capital, capital! Oh, we'll have a column out of this, Mrs Ruggles, a *column*!'

Is he all there, thought Rosie to herself, with his 'sevens' and his 'columns', and wished old Jo would come . . . what was he saying? . . .

'Now, Mrs Ruggles, how about a picture of you all, a Nice Family Group – you and your husband and all the children? – for the paper,' he added, seeing Rosie looked mystified, and he unloaded his box on to the table, rubbed his hands together, and beamed at Mrs Ruggles as if to imply that life could offer nothing more blissful than to be photographed by Mr Walter Wilkins for the *Otwell Gazette*.

Rosie gasped. Photographed! 'You don't mean like this?' she cried, 'in me working clothes and all!'

'Just like that, Mrs Ruggles, *just* like that,' replied Mr Wilkins, who seemed always to repeat his remarks twice over.

Well, thought Rosie, a bit of luck the kids were still in their school clothes and fairly clean, but her and Jo – oh he *did* ought to have given them a bit of notice! And here, thank goodness, *was* Jo!

'Good evening, Mr Ruggles!' cried the journalist, '*good* evening! I'm from the *Otwell Gazette* – been hearing all about your "find" – Mr Short – the author, you know. Come right in,' he cried as Mr Ruggles hesitated on the door step.

Mr Ruggles came in slowly. Summat to do with a re-ward at last was it – well, the bloke seemed to have made himself at home all right – asking him into his own kitchen!

'Now, Mr Ruggles,' said Mr Wilkins, as old Jo shut the door, 'I dare say a few shillings wouldn't come amiss, and I think between us we can make quite a feature of your story, *quite* a feature! Now I want you,' he continued, pausing for breath and producing a notebook, 'to tell me, just in your own words, exactly *how* you found those notes – take your time now, Mr Ruggles – *take* your time,' he added, and smilingly presented Mr Ruggles with a chair. Mr Ruggles sank into it. He felt bewildered. He scratched his head and looked helplessly at Rosie.

'Spit it out, Jo!' she cried encouragingly.

But Mr Ruggles was shy. However, at last, with many promptings from his wife and a lot of encouragement from Mr Wilkins, he was prevailed on to give an account of his adventures. 'You're a born story-teller, Mr Ruggles, a *born* story-teller!' declared Mr Wilkins, patting old Jo on the back when he had finished, and he shut up his little notebook with a click and beamed more than ever.

'And now for the picture!' he cried. 'Pity I can't have your mate Mr Bird in too – no time though – never mind – never mind, he can be "inset" later. Now I think *out-side*,' he continued, leading the way. 'Light bad here. Fine advert. for *you*, Mrs Ruggles,' he added, glancing up at the board over the door – 'you'll have to enlarge the Ideal Laundry after this, I shouldn't wonder! Now, I think *you* seated in the doorway Mr Ruggles, smoking your pipe – you *do* smoke a pipe? – of course! And Mrs Ruggles if *you* could stand beside him – yes – just there – holding the baby; this little girl *here* (he drew Peg forwards) your eldest *here*, and now – let me see – four more – bless my soul, are those twins? – I must make a note of that!' And to the astonishment of Jim and John he pulled out his notebook and rapidly wrote something down. 'You four on the step, my dears,' he said, as he shut up the notebook with a click again. 'That's right. Now just *one* minute while I fetch my camera – don't move!' and he dived into the house and seized his mysterious box off the kitchen table. Well, this *was* a queer go, thought Rosie. What *would* the neighbours say! Ah! there was Mrs 'Nosey Parker' Smith on her doorstep already, and two heads at the window opposite! By the time Mr Wilkins had fixed up his camera and rearranged the Ruggles to his satisfaction, half One End Street had assembled – what *was* going on at No. 1 – Jo Ruggles having his picture took! Coo!

'Now all look at me *one* minute!' cried Mr Wilkins. 'Keep *quite* still . . . *please* would you stand back?' he added, addressing the onlookers. 'Now, one, two . . . *please*, Madam!' as Mrs Smith pushed her way to the front of the crowd. '*Thank* you. Now –!' There was a blinding flash. Rosie nearly dropped William. Mr Ruggles nearly dropped his pipe and everyone blinked.

'Splendid!' cried Mr Wilkins, 'Splendid!' and began rapidly packing up his belongings. 'Good evening, Mr Ruggles, *good* evening, Madam,' he cried, bowing to Rosie, and before the astonished Ruggles could move from their 'group' he had pushed his way through the crowd and disappeared!

'I feels all of a do-da!' exclaimed Mr Ruggles, when at last they had shaken off the inquisitive neighbours and were safely inside the house once again.

'*I* feels like me tea!' said Rosie lifting the kettle off the range. 'Keep your pecker up, old man; one thing's certain, your author-chap's still alive, and where there's life, they says, there's hope!'

The next day every newspaper shop in Otwell displayed posters from the *Otwell Gazette* bearing the words 'Celebrated Author's Luck', and 'Local Man's Amazing Find', and the postman, who seldom troubled the Ruggles, called at No. 1 One End Street with a copy of the *Gazette* ('with the Editor's compliments' printed on the outside), and two letters for Mr Ruggles! Rosie tore open the paper. Coo! There they all were – looking a little startled perhaps, but otherwise as natural as could be . . . and the sign-board and aspidistra and all – you couldn't wish for better! Underneath was printed 'Mr Ruggles with his wife and children; a happy snap at No. 1 One End Street. See page 5. *Inset*, Mr Ruggles's mate. Mr Bird; his son collects stamps', and there, completely filling a small circle, were the head and burly shoulders of Mr Bird!

'What's that in the corner – by your finger, Mum?' asked Kate.

Mrs Ruggles looked more closely. Yes – no – it couldn't be – yes it *was*, a bit of Mrs Smith – her nosey nose actually poked into their photograph – *what* a cheek! . . .

'Listen, Rosie,' interrupted Mr Ruggles who had been busy reading his correspondence, 'seems there's summat in this writing business, tins or no. Here's five shillings been sent me for just sitting in a chair yesterday and telling that gent me doings – and wait a bit,' as Mrs Ruggles made a joyful exclamation. 'here's a letter from the author-bloke hisself, thanking me for my honesty and saying as how he's too busy with work to call at present (think of the five bobs *he's* picking up)! but hopin' to look in next week. He wouldn't surely look in without he meant to bring summat, Rosie – now would he – he'd just keep clear? Hi! stop that hollerin',' he added, as his family began jumping and yelling with excitement, 'the chap may be under a bus, dead of the small-pox or throwed all his money away again by next week! You wait to shout till he's *been*, and keep yer mouths shut, too, outside of here, about the whole business.'

'Hi – Jo,' cried Rosie presently when she had turned to page 5, '*You* never said all this!' For there, under the heading 'Local man's honesty. Riches in a Dustbin', was an account, *not* only of Mr Ruggles's Dust-dump Adventures, but his views on the Weather, the Political Situation, Large Families, the Superiority of Otwell over all other Towns and several other topics! (There was also a long paragraph about 'the Celebrated Author, Mr Short', his tastes and pursuits, and a list of his more famous publications.) 'A column' all right! Mr Ruggles read it.

'Rosie,' he said solemnly when he had finished, 'seems to me there's more than one chap in this Town what gets "ideas in his head"!' and before Mrs Ruggles could think of a suitable retort, he had pocketed the paper and gone off to work.

*

The following Tuesday Mr Ruggles and Mr Bird called as usual at 9 Wistaria Avenue. Was it really only a week since their last visit! Mr Ruggles was shy about going in, and insisted it was his turn to hold the horse, so Mr Bird did the knocking. The author appeared at the window as usual, but instead of throwing out the key, called 'I'm coming down,' and appeared a few minutes later in dressing-gown and pyjamas at the front door, a large bottle of beer in either hand! (Thank Heaven a cheque had come yesterday! He'd completely forgotten this weekly visit; awkward indeed if the busy author had

had to explain there was no money in the house!) Mr
Bird and Mr Ruggles were invited in, and while they
consumed the beer, Mr Short made himself tea on a gas-
ring and opened a tin of sardines. 'My breakfast,' he explained, and Mr Bird had great difficulty in avoiding
Mr Ruggles's eyes.

It was quite a merry meal! Mr Short was always interested in his fellow-creatures, and today he was in a
particularly cheerful mood. Assisted by one of the bottles
of beer, Mr Ruggles completely lost his shyness, and very
soon Mr Short had heard all about Mr Charlie Ruggles,
the Cart Horse Parade, the Risks of Pig Keeping, and
the Price of Allotments.

At last Mr Bird remarked 'as they ought to be movin'
on,' and as Mr Short opened the front door he pressed
something into Mr Ruggles's hand. 'Towards getting to
London, and good luck to you,' he said. Mr Ruggles
gasped. He'd almost forgotten about the reward – all so
matey together! Two quid! *Two quid!* Why, it 'ud pay
for the lot and leave summat over for Bird as well! Charlie and London *at last*! There were tears in his eyes as he
tried to thank 'the bloke'.

'Don't,' said the author; 'I only wish it were more but
times are difficult,' and he slammed the door after his
guests. His cheerful mood had evaporated. Mr Ruggles's
thanks bothered him. Eight human beings (for he supposed the baby was indifferent) achieving complete hap-
piness and their life's ambition for five shillings a head;
five shillings! Thanks . . . Did one pity or envy Mr Ruggles?
Like Lily Rose, Mr Short decided that life was indeed a
puzzle, and pushing aside the 'breakfast' things, he
sank into an arm chair, put his feet on the table, and
lighting a cigarette spent the rest of the morning 'pondering' this problem for the thousandth and fiftieth time.

CHAPTER NINE

Cart Horse Parade

ON Whit Sunday the little Ruggles did an unheard of thing – they attended Sunday School in their Every Day clothes! This startling fact was remarked by Mrs Smith-next-door-but-two ('Nosey Parker') to her husband as they passed by her window.

'Whatever can have happened!' she cried. 'Has their Ma been took bad, do you suppose?'

'More like she's been took *Mad* – 'long of that reward,' replied her husband. 'I've heard of its happening afore now – folks winning Derby Sweeps and such-like; the shock – goes clean to their heads.'

'But it wasn't all *that* much,' objected Mrs Smith. 'I'll just pop in and see if Rosie Ruggles is all right.'

'You'll get no thanks – best leave 'em alone,' said her husband, but Mrs Smith had 'popped' and was already knocking at the door of No. 1.

A strange sight met her eyes when the door was opened; nothing less than Mrs Ruggles in her petticoat and jumper, her hair in curling pins, an iron in her hand, while through a mist of steam and airing clothes could be faintly seen the figure of Mr Ruggles, clothed only in a pair of pants (no better than one of them Nudists you read about, as Mrs Smith said to her husband later) busily engaged in polishing a pair of yellow-brown boots! *What* a spectacle for Sunday afternoon! Mrs Smith's sympathy evaporated and righteous indignation filled her heart.

'Did you want something?' said Rosie coldly.

'I come to see if you was all right,' said Mrs Smith – bravely it must be admitted, for Rosie's looks were anything but inviting. 'I seen the children go by looking –'

she hesitated – 'ahrm – not *quite* like they usually does of a Sunday.'

'*Did* you!' said Rosie. 'And now you see Jo and me not looking quite like *we* usually does of a Sunday either.'

'I do *indeed*,' said Mrs Smith, 'and let me tell you this, Rosie Ruggles – when you come on bad days – and I doubt they won't be far off – treating the Sabbath Day like this – don't come to *me* for help!'

'I shouldn't dream of it,' said Rosie, 'not if it were the Judgement Day itself – *Good* afternoon,' and she shut the door.

'Rosie,' said Mr Ruggles sadly, 'you made An Enemy for Life.'

'Good thing too,' retorted Rosie cheerfully. 'It will be a long time before she puts her nose in this house again – you see.'

*

It was after ten o'clock before the Ruggles's kitchen assumed its normal Sunday evening aspect. Upstairs the little Ruggles lay fast asleep, their clean Sunday clothes beside them ready for the morning's early start.

'Well, Old Man,' said Rosie, as she kissed her husband 'good night'. 'It's come at last – our day to London! Mind you see the alarm's set right – I'd never get over it if we was to miss that train!'

Unfortunately, Mr Ruggles was so unnerved by the awful prospect of over-sleeping, that he set the alarm an hour earlier than he intended, and the entire family was awakened by its piercing clamour at five instead of six.

'Better early than late,' said Rosie philosophically, 'and it will give me more time to cut the sandwiches and see you're dressed proper. You'd all better have breakfast in your underclothes,' she added, 'I don't want no spills and food marks to clean up.'

The little Ruggles thought this was a grand idea but Mr Ruggles objected and compromised by breakfasting in his shirt and trousers. As soon as the meal was over the great business of dressing began in earnest. For a while all went well, even William was subdued and offered no resistance to a yellow woolly suit, woolly boots and a woolly cap with a rakish bobble on top. Then suddenly there was an outcry from Jo, angry shouts and stamps, and at last the sound of muffled tears, mingled with yells of laughter from the twins.

Rosie flew upstairs. 'Whatever are you doing of?' she cried, for there was Jo, standing in the middle of the bedroom, his jersey over his head and face, his arms half in the sleeves, the remainder of which waved wildly in the air. His mother rushed at him and with great difficulty tugged off the jersey. Jo emerged, purple in the face, and roaring with fright and anger to the increased merriment of the twins.

'Be quiet, do,' said Mrs Ruggles, 'can't you see he's half-choked!' It took two glasses of water and many kisses to restore Jo. 'Now try and get into it proper,' said his mother at last, holding up the offending garment, 'it can't have shrunk all that!' But it had! Jo tugged, his mother pulled, and finally with the assistance of Lily Rose and the twins the jersey was *on*, every stitch stretched to its utmost.

'I can't *breve*,' said Jo, swelling himself out like a frog, 'and the sleeves is all wrong!'

'Don't blow-out like that,' said Rosie, 'you'll burst the seams. Here, I'll leave the neck undone, and you can do without a tie; can you breathe now?'

'Better,' said Jo, 'but I'm not going in it.'

'Not going – what do you mean?' said his mother sharply, 'you'll go in that or you won't go at all; there's no more clean jerseys.'

'And you can't get out of it either, without some of us,' giggled John provokingly; Jo scowled at him. It was too true!

'*I can't breve . . . and the sleeves is all wrong!*'

'See he keeps clean,' said Mrs Ruggles to Lily Rose, and hurried off.

Poor Jo! The glory of the great day had departed; here he was, hot, uncomfy, and without even the consolation of his tie, one of his greatest joys! He wriggled and twisted hoping to get more comfortable in his tight garment.

'Be quiet, you'll bust it,' said Lily Rose.

'I *want* to,' replied Jo.

'We'll leave you behind,' said his sister, 'if you're such a naughty boy!'

Jo felt like giving her a good kick or a bite – he was

undecided and pondering which, when, suddenly, he had one of his Ideas. He stopped wriggling, climbed on a chair, and sat quietly, thinking hard.

At last they were all ready and the procession set forth for the station. First came Lily Rose and Kate, looking model little girls in new frocks with flowered bodices and plain skirts, Lily Rose's blue and pink, Kate's green and yellow. (For once in her life, Kate was not wearing one of her sister's 'passed ons' – her frock was indeed her own, having been bought with some of her prize money, and she felt very grand and important.) They wore flowered linen hats that nearly matched their dresses, dark grey stockings and neat brown sandals that rather added to the size of their growing feet.

Lily Rose had a paper 'carrier' in one hand, containing two bottles of milk and a bunch of bananas, and her winter coat, in case of rain, in the other. Kate also had a coat and a small cardboard attaché case in which was her autograph book (who knew what celebrity from Charlie Chaplin to Lady Astor she might not encounter in Regent's Park?) and several ham sandwiches.

The twins, with Peg between them, followed next. Peg was wearing the top half of one of Lily Rose's dresses slightly cut down, an outgrown hat of Kate's, and shoes and socks that had once been Jo's. Her brothers had grey flannel shorts and jerseys of the lovely colours that only come from much washing, much wearing and plenty of sunlight and air; John's pinkish – Jim's a strange blue. Both boys were bareheaded and their red hair glinted in the sun. They also carried coats and bags of food, and Jim had a special ration of sugar he had begged from his mother for his Uncle's horse, 'Bernard Shaw'.

Next came Jo in his tight jersey, and corduroy shorts made from an old pair of Mr Ruggles's trousers. All traces of his tears had disappeared; he smiled to himself and clasped a mysterious brown paper parcel.

Mr and Mrs Ruggles brought up the rear; Rosie very smart in a new artificial silk dress ('navy with a neat floral design' the young women in the shop had described it) and her winter felt hat transformed by three white gardenias from Woolworth's. She carried William in his yellow woollies and a string bag bulging with a great variety of things. Mr Ruggles was in his best suit – black, so as to 'come in' for funerals – but on this occasion livened up by a purple and red pullover with a tie and handkerchief to match. Shiny yellow-brown boots and a well-brushed bowler hat completed his attire, and in his buttonhole he wore a guelder rose or what he called a 'Whitsun boss', which he felt was appropriate to the season. He carried the remainder of the family's coats, and a large fish-frail overflowing with bottles and bags of food.

'You looks fine, Dad,' said Rosie, as she surveyed him proudly before leaving. 'Shouldn't be surprised if you weren't taken for one of the judges theirselves. The only thing what worries me is that split under your right arm – be sure to remember if you waves to anyone to use your left!'

Mr Ruggles promised and told his wife *she* looked 'a fair treat'.

As they passed No. 4, Mrs Ruggles suddenly became engrossed with William, but Mr Ruggles looked straight at the house and declared he saw 'Nosey Parker' peeping round a corner of the blind!

At the station Jo bought the tickets and was delighted to find that on Bank Holidays children up to fourteen were allowed half price.

The ticket-clerk eyed Lily Rose suspiciously and said

she was a fine grown girl, and Mrs Ruggles said 'Yes, wasn't she' and perhaps he would like one of them to run home and fetch the birth certificate? The clerk made no reply to these pleasantries, dismissed William as 'in arms' and they all got into the train.

The Ruggles family took up an entire carriage; Mr and Mrs Ruggles, Lily Rose and Kate in the four corners, the rest in between!

'Now enjoy yourselves, but keep quiet,' said Rosie firmly. 'Here's a banana each, and three comics between the lot of you,' she added, diving into the string bag and extracting the fruit and copies of *The Rainbow*, *Comic Cuts*, and *The Chicks' Own*.

Mr Ruggles opened his eyes wide at this piece of extravagance. '*Three* papers! you have been going a bust!' he said.

'Sixpence,' replied his wife, 'and well worth it; it's an invest*ment* – you'll see!'

She was right. During the whole journey to London, lasting nearly an hour and a half, the children were perfectly good. For most of them it was their first trip in a train and this alone was sufficient to keep them quiet and interested. But after a time their eyes got tired of looking at the quickly moving trees and fields and telegraph wires – the latter rising, rising till you felt they would disappear altogether when suddenly, 'plop' – something seemed to hit them down again. And then, as the trees and fields gave place to small towns and the outlook became more familiar and less exciting, they were glad to have the 'comics' and remained immersed in these until it was clear London was in sight. Even William obliged by sleeping peacefully, considerately waking just before they arrived.

On the platform at Victoria Station stood Mr Ruggles's

sister-in-law, Mrs Charlie Ruggles (Auntie Ivy). 'You've never brought *William*!' she exclaimed joyfully when all her relations were safely out of the train, 'Oh, ain't he sweet!' and William was smothered in kisses and about to protest with one of his famous yells, when an engine let off such a shriek that he felt discouraged and merely gurgled instead.

'Charlie's at the Park with the cart and horse,' continued Auntie Ivy, who spoke very fast and seemed to have a great deal to say. 'The children's there too with my sister Mrs Perkins and her kids – you haven't met her, have you, Rosie – husband's in the carpentry business – cabinet maker he is; thinks he's a bit above Dustmen but I tells him there's not much difference between saw-dust and other dust as I can see, and anyway, he's glad enough to come and ride in our cart today! Come along now, we mustn't stand talking here,' she continued, 'the first parade round's at half past nine and you'd like to see Uncle before he starts – he's hoping you'll go with him?' she added, turning to old Jo.

The little Ruggles looked at each other at this remark, but only Jim had the courage to put into words the thought that had occurred to each of them. 'But aren't we *all* going!' he asked, his eyes big with apprehension.

'Why, bless your heart, yes,' replied Auntie Ivy, patting him on the head, which he detested, 'but you see it's like this. The carts all go round for the Judging first – long time they takes and tedious it is waiting – specially if you're far back in the line – six hundred and thirty-first we was last year. No, when *we* all go is in the Grand Parade in the afternoon; only the carts what's won first prizes go *then* – *anyone* can go in the morning!'

'But how do you *know* you'll win a first prize?' persisted Jim. Horrible thought! Suppose Uncle Charlie *didn't* then they'd none of them, except Dad apparently, be 'in' any Parade at all! And Jim had visions of the Black Hand Gang and how they would laugh, for he and John had boasted a great deal about how they were going to London and of the Grand Parade in which they were to take part.

'Don't talk stupid,' said Rose sharply; 'your uncle always wins first prizes.'

'That's so,' said Auntie Ivy, smiling good-temperedly. 'Don't you be afraid; Uncle's had first prizes for eleven years – every time he's entered except last year, and that were bad luck along of the horse spraining his leg; there's nothing wrong with Bernard Shaw this year – he looks a treat and no mistake – all dressed up like a dog's dinner! Now, come along all.'

'Hang on to your Dad, Peg and Jo,' commanded Rosie, 'and the rest of you, don't lose sight of your Auntie for *one* minute.'

The little Ruggles did their best but it was difficult to keep Mrs Charlie's swiftly moving form in view, and at the same time take in the glories of Victoria Station, the queer tiled passage to the Underground railway and the funny electric underground trains themselves. However, they all got safely into one mysteriously labelled 'Inner Circle', and sat silently staring with all their eyes.

The train was very hot and very noisy; it rattled through tunnels and lurched into stations, coming to a stop with a fearful wailing and shrieking of brakes, and then, just as you were getting used to the comparative quiet and about to make a remark to your neighbour, off it started again! No one but Auntie Ivy would have attempted to keep up a conversation against its deafening roar, but she smilingly shouted away to Rosie, who nodded her head at intervals to intimate she had heard

some thrilling piece of family gossip. At every station
people poured *in* but none, alas, poured *out*; the train
became hotter and hotter and fuller and fuller. Lily Rose
took Peg on her lap to make more room and Auntie Ivy
smilingly patted her knees in invitation to Jo who sat
opposite her. But Jo shook his head. Sitting on anyone's
knee he considered much beneath his dignity and it was
only after his Father, who had stood up to give his seat to
a fat woman with a baby and half her flower garden in
her arms, roared at him above the din to 'get up at once
and sit on Auntie' that he reluctantly tottered across the
swaying train.

'What's in the parcel?' shouted his aunt, as she lifted
him on her lap, but Jo made no reply. You might be
forced to sit on someone's knee but surely no one could
blame you if you didn't hear right what people said in
that noise!

'Next stop ours,' screamed Auntie Ivy a few minutes
later. Rosie nodded and peered round the standing pas-
sengers to impart the good news to her husband. Oh
dear! There was old Jo 'strap-hanging' by his wrong arm
– the split had increased by at least 2 inches, and was
spreading rapidly! Thank Heaven the next stop was
theirs!

Once out of Baker St Station, which was bewildering
with people rushing and pushing in every direction, progress was calmer, but still hot and exhausting. 'Stoking
up,' said Mr Ruggles cheerfully, and prophesied that the
day would be a regular scorcher.

At last they reached an entrance to the Park and there
was a chorus of 'oo's' and 'oh's' and 'there-they-ares'
from the family, and 'sure-'nuff', as Mr Ruggles said,
there 'they' were!

There seemed to be hundreds and hundreds of carts

and horses of all kinds drawn up in a line that stretched
far out of sight. Coal Carts, Drays, Railway Vans, Brew-
ers' Wagons, and last, but certainly not least, Dust Carts:
and dust carts of every description, and all – horses and
carts – looking more like something out of the most ex-
pensive toy-shop than anything in real life!

'Just look at 'em!' cried Rosie, bouncing William up
and down in her excitement, 'that big black horse – ain't
he a marvel – and that pair there with the poppies round
their necks – the *shine* on 'em!'

The drivers sat proud and smiling, holding their whips
decorated with round cardboard discs representing prizes
they had won in previous years; some had only one or
two, others a dozen or so; several of the old men had so
many that their whips were covered from handle to lash.
'Hi – Jo!' called Rosie, 'what would you and your old
boy look like among this lot!' But Mr Ruggles was past
speech and busy looking out for his brother.

'You wait till you see Bernard Shaw,' said Auntie
Ivy, who seemed to know many of the competitors and
shouted good luck messages of encouragement as she
passed, 'and there he is!' The procession which had been
moving very slowly came to a temporary stop and from
a cart just ahead a man wildly waved his whip at them.
Mrs Charlie ran forward and took the reins from her husband, who jumped down to greet his relations.

Uncle Charlie was in gala dress! Decorated with a
pink geranium peeping coyly from behind his left ear,
a cloth cap was perched on the back of his head, his wavy
hair curling over the peak in a plumy crest, while a
short-sleeved yellow shirt with a magenta scarf round the
throat, dark trousers and white tennis shoes completed
his gay attire. He was a striking contrast to his brother-
in-law the cabinet maker, Mr Leslie Perkins, who sat in

the cart smoking a cigarette, and who wore a severe looking black suit and bowler hat – a yellow rose in his button-hole his only attempt at brightness.

Uncle Charlie shook hands vigorously with his brother, slapping him three times on the back for luck, gave Rosie a resounding kiss, almost knocking off her hat and seriously displacing one of the white gardenias, shook hands with his nephews and nieces remembering all their names correctly and made acquaintance with Peg and William for the first time by playfully pinching their noses.

Leaning against the railings and looking resigned and as if she had been there some time, was Mrs Perkins – 'your Auntie Mabel,' said Mrs Charlie introducing her. Mrs Perkins wore a brown and pink flowered silk dress, an unopened parasol hung on her arm, and in her neatly gloved hands she held a fancy basket decorated with raffia and woolwork, containing her own and her family's lunch. Beside her stood her two children, Anthony aged seven, attired in a brown velvet pinafore suit and Pamela aged nine wearing a pink silk frock with flounces to the waist, a hat with daisies, and (to the astonishment and secret scorn of Lily Rose and Kate) what had been, when she left home, white cotton gloves! Altogether a very refined group and one to which I am sorry to say most of the Ruggles took an immediate dislike!

'And where's your kids, Ivy?' demanded Mrs Ruggles, when introductions to the Perkins family were over. Uncle Charlie laughed and shouted, 'Pull up the blinds!' and in a twinkling the sides of the dust cart which had appeared to be covered in with canvas, flew up and dozens of children's laughing faces peeped out.

'Good as a conjuring trick!' laughed old Jo, while Rosie said it put her in mind of the old woman in a shoe!

'Which is yours, Ivy?' she asked, 'and who's all the others – do they belong to Auntie Mabel here?'

'Certainly not,' said Mrs Perkins stiffly. 'I have only Anthony and Pamela.'

'Sorry, I'm sure,' said Rosie, 'but you see I'm used to large families.'

'They're neighbours' children,' explained Mrs Charlie,

Anthony and Pamela

'here's mine' – as two girls and two boys detached themselves from the others and with some difficulty climbed out of the cart. 'You've seen the twins, May and Doris, and Frankie,' she added, pushing forward two girls of ten and a boy of nine, 'and this is Elfred – you've not seen him since he were William's size,' and she indicated a stout lad of six with a grin from ear to ear.

While Rosie was embracing her nephews and nieces, who were singularly untidy, not to say grubby, and commenting on the remarkable growth of Elfred, Uncle Charlie was busy unloading the remaining children, for the procession was about to move on again. 'Off with you!' he cried. 'Come back at one o'clock, and if I've a first prize round we'll go!'

The children ran off and Jo, Rosie and the little Ruggles all crowded round the decorated cart and Bernard Shaw.

Bernard Shaw was indeed 'a treat' – 'all dressed up like a dog's dinner!' His black satiny coat shone and gleamed like a well-kept blackleaded stove. His feathery pasterns had been washed and carefully brushed and combed, his shoes stained and polished. But the triumph of his toilet was his mane and tail ('Took three hours that did,' said Auntie Ivy proudly). These were plaited in a most intricate manner with raffia and green and orange braid, little tufts of raffia standing upright at intervals. Round his neck was a garland of orange paper roses and emerald leaves, and the same colour scheme was carried out with more braid and roses along the shafts and harness. Every particle of brass gleamed and twinkled in the sun, and ten of the round brass medals given every year to first prize horses by the R.S.P.C.A. made a brave show jingling gaily from his breast as he walked. The cart, a modern kind with rubber wheels, had been newly painted, had fresh canvas 'slats', and smelt, Mr Ruggles declared, 'like three hospitals and a surgery in one'; Uncle Charlie said he was glad to hear it, and so it ought, for he'd wasted six penn'orth of disinfectant on it.

Bernard Shaw neighed and tossed his head, and began to stamp impatiently.

'They're off again,' said Uncle Charlie. 'He knows.'

It was true, the long line of carts had begun to move. 'Jump up, Jo,' cried Uncle Charlie, and Mr Ruggles

climbed nimbly into the cart. His brother touched
Bernard Shaw lightly with his whip with the ten red and
one blue round discs, and they moved off. Mr Ruggles
waved – ('Hi – Jo, wrong arm!' cried Rosie). 'Good-bye
– all,' called Mr Perkins sedately, removing his cigarette
from his lips, 'Good-bye, Good luck!' shouted the two
Mrs Ruggles together. 'Good luck,' echoed all the children – even Auntie Mabel Perkins could be seen murmuring something and waving one of her neatly gloved hands.

*

'And what's the programme now?' said Rosie when
two or three dozen carts had passed by, and Bernard
Shaw was a small speck in the distance. 'I'd be glad to
sit down a bit – William's no light weight, I can tell you!'

'*I* feel ready to drop,' said Mrs Perkins – 'I think a
chair in the shade would be very pleasant – those green
ones over there out of the crowd looks nice,' and she
pointed to some deck chairs under the trees near the Lake.

'We've got about two hours afore they'll be back,' said
Auntie Ivy, when she and her sisters-in-law had settled
themselves comfortably in the chairs a few minutes later,
'now what about the kids?' For the six Ruggles, all
clasping their coats and bags, her own four untidy girls
and boys and their two tidy cousins, stood in a group
waiting for instructions and casting longing eyes towards
the Lake which was covered with little boats.

'That boy of yours looks hot,' said Mrs Perkins in-
dicating Jo. 'His jersey's a little tight, isn't it?'

'He grows so fast,' answered Rosie – 'big boy for seven
he is; now your Anthony – you'd never think they was
the same age, now would you?'

'No,' said Mrs Perkins, she wouldn't, 'nor cousins
neither,' she added darkly.

Rosie agreed.

'They can't play here,' said Mrs Perkins, 'not near that lake – much too dangerous!'

'There's a Play Park over to the left,' said Auntie Ivy, who had been looking about, 'they'd better go there – that's safe enough.'

'Oh, such *rough* children in those places,' objected Mrs Perkins, 'and *you never know what your own won't pick up*; I r*ee*ly think I'd rather Anthony and Pam*e*la played quietly here under the trees!'

'Oh, don't be silly, Mabel!' cried Auntie Ivy. 'A couple of hours with rough children won't hurt them, and as to picking things up, it's no good being too particular on Bank Holiday – come to that, I thought I felt something nip me in the train.'

'It's not so much *those*,' replied Mrs Perkins, lowering her voice, 'as *germs*!'

'Oh, germs be bothered!' cried Rosie – 'our kids looks healthy enough, and it's all outside – not like cinemas – let Pam*e*la keep her gloves on if you're so particular!'

'Certainly not,' retorted Auntie Mabel, 'those are her *best* gloves.'

'Well, there'll be no peace if my children stay here,' said Rosie, 'they'll be in that lake in two minutes; it's the Play Park, rough children and germs or not, for them.'

Auntie Ivy said it was the same for hers, and after some arguing Mrs Perkins was prevailed on to agree. Even then it was some time before the children started, so many were the instructions for their welfare and behaviour – particularly that of the little Perkins!

'Don't go near the sand-pits, either of you,' said their mother. 'Don't speak to strangers and remember, if any speaks to you what I always tells you to say – "Mother's watching us, thank you!" *Don't* go near the Giant Stride,

Pamela,' she continued, 'or you'll tear your frock, and Anthony, you mustn't go on the chute – it'll ruin those velvet breeches. Only *one* ice each mind, and Pamela, don't buy Rock – you know it always makes you sick. *Don't . . .*'

'Well, if they remembers all that, Mabel,' interrupted Auntie Ivy, 'they ought to have their photos in the paper – model children,' she added, seeing her sister-in-law looked puzzled. 'Now *you* show your cousins how nice *you* can behave,' she said, addressing her own family, 'and don't stir out of that Play Park till I comes to fetch you all!'

'And you behave *your*selves,' said Rosie, turning to her children. '*No, you can't go in those boats,*' she added, after persistent entreaties from the twins. 'If your father likes to take you, when he comes back, well and good; you're not going *now*. Lily Rose, be sure and keep an eye on Peg and Jo, and try and keep clean the lot of you, do. Now off you all go!'

'Remember, Pamela,' called Mrs Perkins, 'don't –'

But she spoke to empty air! Pamela was a faint pink streak in the far distance!

CHAPTER TEN

The Perfect Day

IT certainly did not seem as if nearly two hours had gone by (so quickly does the time go, discussing the virtues and vices – particularly the vices – of one's relatives) when the three sisters-in-law saw old Jo coming towards them.

'Back already!' cried Auntie Ivy – 'Well, I never – quick! tell us all about it!'

'Fine it was!' said Mr Ruggles, 'slow going at times and phew! hot's not the word, but *fine*! Charlie's got his First all right, and one of the judges commended Bernard Shaw special. Now what about a little bit of grub, Rosie; they're waiting over there by the railings – and where's the kids?'

'They're safe in the Play Park,' said Auntie Ivy. 'I'll fetch 'em,' and she set off.

Auntie Ivy seemed away a long time.

'Oh, dear!' said Mrs Perkins, 'I hope nothing's happened, I'm sure – two hours is a long time, but I got so interested in that story about Ivy's brother-in-law and the people next door, and what the doctor said about Uncle Percy's inside.'

'Why, I see our Jim down there,' said Mr Ruggles, 'that's his red head I'll swear – there – in that crowd by the Lake!'

'Here, take William!' cried Rosie, 'while I go and see – that's him all right,' she added, 'and there's Kate and there –' she gasped – 'there's Peg – *with a Policeman* – oh my goodness me!' and off she flew.

As Mrs Ruggles neared the crowd, Kate ran to meet her. 'Oo, Mum, come quick!' she cried, pulling her mother by the hand and stuttering in her excitement. 'P – Pamela's in the Lake and a p-policeman says our Peg's been s-stealing!'

'Oh, my goodness me!' cried Mrs Ruggles again, pushing her way into the crowd.

Sure enough, there was Peg, howling in the arms of a policeman, and Pamela, not in the Lake, but dripping on land and howling too, while Lily Rose and a Park-keeper did their best to wring the water out of her pink silk flounces!

'Whatever have you been doing of – are all the rest of

you safe?' cried poor Mrs Ruggles looking wildly round.
Yes, there they all were, the twins and Frankie Ruggles
looking sheepish, Anthony, his velvet suit torn and dusty,
and his forehead decorated with a large black bruise,
swelling visibly; May and Doris dirtier and untidier than
before and Elfred, wet and muddy, but still grinning
from ear to ear. All there except Jo!

There was Peg, howling in the arms of a policeman

'Where's Jo?' she cried.

'He's all right, Mum,' said Lily Rose, pausing in her
drying operations, 'he's in the Park – I left him on a
swing.'

'This your little girl?' inquired the policeman, indi-
cating Peg. 'You'd better teach her she can't pick flowers
in Public Parks,' he added sternly, and deposited the
howling Peg in her mother's arms; to her horror Mrs
Ruggles beheld a large bunch of choice pink roses in one
of Peg's fat hands. 'She never done such a thing before!'

cried Rosie indignantly, 'Stop that noise,' she added, giving her daughter a shake, 'and tell the policeman so!'

But the policeman had lost interest and merely shrugged his shoulders, and called to the crowd in general to 'move along there, move along.'

'*This* your child?' inquired the Park-keeper pointing to the still dripping Pamela.

'No!' snapped Rosie, 'she's *not*. What you done, you naughty girl – my word, won't your Ma have a fit – you'd better take that frock right off and dry it in the sun,' she continued, 'you'll never get it dry like that!'

'Oh, oh!' wept Pamela, 'it's my best frock!'

'I don't care what frock it is,' cried Mrs Ruggles, 'take it off her, Lily Rose, or she'll catch her death – and look at your *feet* – oh, my goodness me – and where's your hat?'

'*I've* got it, Auntie,' cried Frankie Ruggles proudly, and he held up a dripping object on the end of a stick, '*I* saved it!'

By this time Auntie Ivy and Mrs Perkins had arrived on the scene. 'I knew something would happen!' cried Auntie Mabel tearfully, 'I felt it! And to think I sat there listening about your brother-in-law and Uncle Percy's inside while my little Pamela was nearly drowned! Oh dear! What can I do with her now, she can't walk across the Park like that, half dressed! And little Anthony! Just look at his forehead and not a bit of butter handy!'

'Oh, don't talk silly, Mabel!' cried Auntie Ivy. 'Pamela's all right – not even a quarter drowned as anyone could tell by the noise she's making, and if she walked about in her vest only, no one 'ud notice or care if they did – and Anthony's all right – he'll have many a worse bruise than that afore he's done! I'm sorry I'm sure it's

happened, tho' what they've been doing of I don't know
– didn't I tell you not to stir from that Play Park?' she
added, seizing Doris by the arm and giving her a little
shake.

There was a chorus of explanations.

'Well; *I* can't wait to hear,' cried Mrs Ruggles.

'I've *got it, Auntie!*' cried Frankie Ruggles, 'I *saved it!*'

'Here, Kate, keep hold of Peg and don't let her touch
another flower. I'm off to fetch Jo – goodness knows
what *he*'s up to by this time!' and she hurried away.

Once in the Play Park Mrs Ruggles looked anxiously
about – 'Left him on the swing' Lily Rose had said, but
how long ago was that! She went from one group to

another, but there was no sign of the fat little figure in the tight green jersey. She was just thinking of asking the Play Park attendant if she had noticed any child answering to Jo's description, when suddenly from above her, a voice called out 'Hullo, Mum, is it dinner time?' and looking up Mrs Ruggles saw a figure perched on top of the Chute just preparing to take a slide down, head first! Jo, certainly, but no longer in the tight green jersey, but comfortably attired in what his mother immediately recognized as a very old, torn and dirty garment belonging to Jim!

'Come down at once,' cried Mrs Ruggles. Never had she been so quickly obeyed! She had hardly spoken the words before Jo was at her feet – head first. He looked a strange little object. The jersey reached almost to his knees when he stood up – but he had rolled up the sleeves, and looked supremely comfortable. Mrs Ruggles seized him by the arm. 'Where did you get that jersey?' she demanded angrily.

'I brought it,' replied Jo, smiling sweetly, but looking at his mother out of the corner of his eyes. 'It's Jim's,' he added. 'I was too hot in mine!'

'So *that's* what you had in the parcel!' cried Mrs Ruggles, 'and where's your own, may I ask, and how in the name of fortune did you get out of it by yourself, answer me that!'

'The boys "skinned" me,' said Jo, avoiding the first question.

'I'll skin you!' cried Mrs Ruggles – 'answer my question – where's your own jersey?' Jo made no reply. 'Come now, you tell me where it is or it's no dinner you'll get,' said Mrs Ruggles firmly.

'I give it away,' muttered Jo at length.

'You *what*!' cried Mrs Ruggles.

'I *give* it away,' repeated Jo sulkily. 'It wasn't no good!'

Mrs Ruggles was almost speechless with anger – given away – a good jersey like that – ready for Peg in a year or so, not to mention William!

'And who *to*, may I ask?' she demanded furiously.

'Oh, a lady,' said Jo vaguely. 'I put it on a seat and she said I didn't seem to want it and could she have it – fit her little boy nice. *I* didn't want it. She gave me a penny,' he added proudly.

'I'll give you something when we get home!' cried Mrs Ruggles. 'Show me the lady – quick!'

But it was no good, look where they might, the lady had vanished.

'Be quiet!' said Mrs Ruggles sharply to the now-weeping Jo. 'As if it weren't bad enough to have you looking like summat off a dust heap without that hollering – making everyone look at you!' But Jo only wept the louder. 'Any more of it,' said his mother, 'and you don't go in the Procession!'

Jo's tears stopped as if by magic. Uncle Charlie *had* got a First then! By the time they reached the railings where Bernard Shaw was drawn up he was almost cheerful again, and only giving vent to an occasional sniff. Certainly the proceedings going on round the cart were sufficient to make anyone completely cheer up! Spread just inside the railings on the grass was a huge white tablecloth covered with the contents of all the various bags and baskets – a wonderful array of food and drink – while the whole party sat round singing at the top of their voices, to Uncle Charlie's accompaniment on a mouth organ, 'Pack up your troubles in your old kit bag!' Extraordinary transformation! Really – thought Mrs Ruggles, if it were not for seeing Pamela sitting there in her petticoat, her dress and Lily Rose's hat hanging on the railings to dry, she'd have thought the last hour was all a dream – or rather a nightmare!

'Come on, Rosie, old girl!' cried Uncle Charlie waving the mouth-organ, 'we're all starving and only waiting for you and the boy to begin!'

In spite of her anger about the jersey and Jo's appearance (upon which she could hear comments from Mrs Perkins), Mrs Ruggles was starving too (was it really only this morning she'd cut these sandwiches – seemed like last week!) and thankful to see everything ready.

'You all seems cheerful enough, anyway,' she said in a relieved voice as she sat down.

'That's my little song,' said Uncle Charlie, 'nothing like music for cheering one up – and it weren't altogether the kids' fault,' he added, lowering his voice and jerking his head towards the garments on the railings, 'Ivy'll tell you.'

But Mrs Ruggles felt it was wiser to avoid the subject at present, and it was not until the meal was over and everyone feeling almost too full of ham and doughnuts and ginger-beer to move – even Uncle Charlie quiescent – stretched full length on the grass with a newspaper over his head to keep off the sun and flies – that she heard what had really happened and how it was not 'altogether the kids' fault'.

*

'It seems,' said Auntie Ivy, 'as that lake goes through the Play Park too, and, of course, the kids made straight for it – all but Peg and Jo, who were busy on the swings and didn't spot it. While they was there watching the boats, up comes a lady and says if your twins, Rosie, 'ull stand still for five minutes while she draws 'em, she'll give 'em a ride on the water – attracted by their fiery

heads it seems she were! Anyway, she did a sketch of 'em
and gives 'em some money for a ride. Of course, all the
others wanted to go too, and in the end she packed the
lot into a boat. Pamela was a bit nervous, Kate said, but
the lady she said she'd stand on the bank and see as they
was all right and off they went. All went well till time was
nearly up, then Lily Rose there's hat blew off and trying
to fish it out they all crowded to one side of the boat –
course far too many in it – and Pamela overbalanced and
went in head first! Luckily they was round this part of
the lake by then and close to the edge where the water's
only about a foot deep, and a Park-keeper had her out in
a jiffy! But you can't really blame 'em – Bank Holiday
and a free trip and all – might as well blame Rosie
here for having redheaded boys – If it hadn't been for
that it 'ud probably never have happened! (How your
Peg got in the flower beds, Rosie, I've *not* heard – just
wandered off on her own, I suppose – anyway she's
picked you some nice roses!)'

'I'm blaming no one,' said Mrs Perkins, 'except the
artist-lady who should have knowed better; people didn't
ought to interfere with other people's children – sketching 'em in a public place too!'

'You wouldn't say that if it were your kids what had
been sketched,' said Mrs Ruggles sharply; 'and where
did she get to, Ivy – I never seed no artist about?'

'Doris said,' replied Auntie Ivy, 'as a gentleman friend
come along while they was on the water, and the lady
just waved her sketching book at 'em, shouted good-bye,
and went off with him.'

'And that was seeing they was all right, I suppose!'
said Mrs Perkins grimly. 'You can't trust artists. There
was a sign painter at Leslie's works . . .' But what the sign
painter did or did not do was never revealed, for the

'neighbours' children' (and a great many others with them) came running up, calling 'Please, Mr Ruggles, one o'clock!'

Uncle Charlie removed the newspaper, sat up, and drew a large watch from his pocket. 'So it is!' he cried. 'Pack up, quick, they'll be starting in a jiffy!'

'Oh dear!' said Mrs Perkins, 'I wonder if Pamela's frock's dry – she *can't* go like that!' Yes, it was dry all

'*Please, Mr Ruggles, one o'clock!*'

right, but alas! had shrunk 'something terrible' – a whole flounce shorter at least!

'Artificial silk!' said Rosie knowingly – 'it *does* do queer things sometimes!' and she looked at Lily Rose, who blushed and giggled and became very busy putting on her newly dried hat which fortunately had *not* shrunk.

'Now how many are we?' said Uncle Charlie, and began counting the party. Eight Ruggles, not counting William, Four Perkins, Six of themselves, old Mr and Mrs Buckle-from-next-door, who hadn't arrived yet, and apparently about two dozen 'neighbours' children'! He began sorting them out, 'only the ten what came this morning,' he said firmly, 'that makes us thirty, and enough for Bernard Shaw or any other horse!'

It was a great business loading up, but at last they were all settled. Uncle Charlie and old Jo sat on the box, while Mr and Mrs Buckle (who had been almost given up and arrived just as they were about to start, and had to be hoisted up by interested spectators to cries of 'oh, my rheumatics, mind my pore legs' from Mrs Buckle), the Perkins, Auntie Ivy, and Rosie with William on her lap, were accommodated on a bench placed at the back of the cart. 'A tight squash,' remarked Auntie Ivy, 'but all the better should Bernard Shaw take it into his head to do something strange.'

'*Will* he?' asked Mrs Perkins fearfully.

'Now how should I know, Mabel,' replied Auntie Ivy – 'he's shied once or twice when he's been excited, that's all I've ever *known* him do. I was just thinking he might –'

'*What?*' said Mrs Perkins, but Auntie Ivy had seen a friend in the crowd, and was busy exchanging greetings. The children were all lined up on either side of the cart, the 'slats' pulled up as far as possible, and there was a perfect view for everyone. The cart in front began to move forward. Bernard Shaw threw up his head and neighed loudly; the onlookers cheered, they were off – the Grand Parade had begun!

*

How thrilling it all was! Jim and John pinched each other in their excitement – something to tell the Gang all right! How superior one felt looking down on all those people in the waving, cheering crowd, and how pleasant to hear the flattering remarks 'passed' on Bernard Shaw's appearance! Even Uncle Charlie came in for some of the applause, but whether for himself and his gala attire or the splendour of his cart and horse it was hard to decide. He acknowledged it all, smiling and waving and had an apt reply for every remark, for Uncle Charlie loved any kind of public speaking, attended a working men's college three nights a week with a view to what he called 'taking it up political', and welcomed any opportunity for practice.

Although they had started punctually at half past one it was over an hour before they even came in sight of the Judges' stand and another twenty minutes before they reached it. It was very hot and the sun beat fiercely down. Mrs Perkins tried to put up her parasol, but the spikes kept catching in Mrs Buckle's hat or endangering William's eyes, and she sighed and gave up the attempt. Mr Perkins sighed too, and said at this rate they'd be shockingly late home and long after Anthony's bedtime. Auntie Ivy remarked it was an extra large entry this year, adding cheerfully that their cart seemed rather far back in the line, while old Mr Buckle, who was a retired coal-cart driver and had taken part in processions for over thirty years, was 'put in mind' of how he had once been last but three, and his horse had dropped from exhaustion when they eventually arrived home just after two in the morning!

However, at last they reached the Judges' stand, and Uncle Charlie bent forward to receive his prize from a very grand lady in flowing grey robes, with scarlet lips and nails to match, who congratulated him, remarked on his fine horse and inquired its name.

'*Really*!' she said, when she heard it, raising her plucked eyebrows, 'now, *why*?'

'Because though he's an old horse, lady,' replied Uncle Charlie, 'he's a dark horse, and one's never sure what he'll do next!' And, as if to confirm this statement,

Bernard Shaw suddenly reared – threw up his head, threw up his heels and *bolted*!

Auntie Mabel screamed, William let forth one of his famous yells, Mrs Buckle cried, 'oh, my pore legs,' while Mr Buckle was 'put in mind' of an occasion in 1910 (or was it '11?) when a friend's horse had done the very same thing and everyone was thrown out and in hospital a week! Only the children really enjoyed it, flung together in a heap at the bottom of the cart. Jim and John even managed to pinch each other – adventures all right!

It was soon over; two men rushed forward and seized the bridle and Bernard Shaw subsided immediately, and though the party on the bench were slightly shaken, no one was hurt, being, as Auntie Ivy had said, too tightly wedged for much damage. Tempers, however, were not improved, and it was still a long time before the Procession would be out of the Park. The Perkins began suggesting they should be put out as time was going and they had a long way to get home.

'What! go home at three o'clock on Bank Holiday!' exclaimed Uncle Charlie. 'Ivy and I'll be thinking you haven't enjoyed yourselves – why, we haven't begun the day yet! Jo here and I, we've got a little surprise for you – instead of tea in the Park at one of them stalls like we'd arranged, how about a Regular Blow Out in a Posh Tea Shop – does that appeal to any of you?'

It did. It appealed to all. Complete harmony was restored and in less than five minutes they were all singing (unaccompanied this time, for Uncle Charlie declared he must keep all his attention on Bernard Shaw after his recent behaviour) 'For he's a jolly good fellow'.

'What made you tell the lady that yarn about Bernard Shaw?' inquired Old Jo presently, for he knew well enough the horse was called 'Bernard' after its last driver, the 'Shaw' having been added by Uncle Charlie 'for a joke'. But Uncle Charlie only laughed and refused to give his reasons.

It was after four o'clock by the time their part of the procession had reached the road again, the 'neighbours' children' reluctantly dismissed, and the whole party un-loaded to await Uncle Charlie's return from stabling his horse. A very happy arrangement it appeared had been made in regard to this. Mr Buckle's son, chauffeur to a doctor in the district and out driving all day, had 'for a consideration' as he called it, kindly given permission for Bernard Shaw to be temporarily stabled in his employer's garage and Uncle Charlie gaily waved the key as he drove off! He was soon back, and in less than an hour they were all sitting, rather bewildered by the rapid transport of buses and lifts, the crowded room, the lights and the music, round two big tables in one of Lyons's largest and most 'Posh' tea shops, a gentleman in even-ing dress bowing before them, while a waitress like a film star stood at his side awaiting their instructions!

Bewildering was the word! Everyone felt a little over-come by so much grandeur – all except Mrs Perkins who, completely unembarrassed by the bows of the gentleman in evening dress, and the aloof expression on the face of the film-star waitress, sat down and removed her gloves as calmly as if she had tea in these surroundings every day!

For a while it seemed no one was going to be able to summon up sufficient courage to order anything, and the waitress was beginning to show signs of impatience, when Mr Perkins surprisingly announced that *he* would like to make a little contribution to the party, and how about a Sundae all round to begin with? None of the Ruggles was quite sure what a sundae was, while old Mr and Mrs Buckle most certainly had no idea: only Mr

Buckle, however, was courageous enough to say so, and though one was ready for almost anything on Bank Holiday, it was reassuring to hear it was only a very superior kind of ice cream. Everyone said yes, please, and Mr Perkins gave the order with an air of calm detachment, as if ordering twenty sundaes at a blow was quite an everyday occurrence!

'What they do get up for money!' exclaimed old Mrs Buckle, when the delicacies eventually arrived, while Mr Buckle, after a spoonful or two, remarked (which was neither tactful nor polite), that, in his opinion, they didn't come up to the old-fashioned ice cream cornet. He was just being put in mind of some story connected with ices, when the orchestra struck up 'Men of Harlech', Uncle Charlie held up a warning finger, cried '*There's* music for you; listen to that!' and he subsided and, equal to an old-fashioned cornet or not, lapped up the remainder of his sundae with apparent enjoyment.

*

Tea was over. Replete with food, and, truth to tell, a little drowsy from the overheated room and the soothing strains of the orchestra, the party were lolling quietly in their chairs. Mrs Buckle, her rheumatics forgotten, was frankly nodding, while her husband, if he was put in mind of anything, was keeping it quietly to himself. Even the children were silent. Only Uncle Charlie remained undaunted, and lovingly fingering his mouth organ, whispered to his brother, did he think the orchestra would mind if he, Charlie, were to join in? Mr Ruggles looked alarmed, while Auntie Mabel, who had overheard the remark, said nervously that she hoped he wouldn't do nothing conspicuous, adding, as the applause for 'Men of Harlech' came to an end, that she did wish as they'd play that beautiful piece, 'My Heart's Desire'. 'They plays it at the Arcadia Tea House, near us,' she said turning to Rosie. 'Leslie and I, we go there for supper sometimes,' she explained (so *that* was why Auntie Mabel was so at home in surroundings like this, and why Uncle Leslie knew all about sundaes! A reason for most things if you only knew it, thought Rosie to herself), and she smiled sleepily at Auntie Mabel and said supper out must make a nice change for Leslie ... and what was Uncle Charlie up to *now*? For Uncle Charlie was making his way among the tables towards the orchestra!

'I believe he *is* going to join in!' cried Auntie Ivy, for her husband was speaking to the conductor. But no! He was coming back, the conductor was bowing in their direction, and the next minute the orchestra struck up 'My Heart's Desire'!

'Oh, Charlie!' exclaimed Auntie Mabel, as he sat down, 'however did you make them do it!'

Uncle Charlie looked wise. 'I suppose the conductor liked my face,' he replied, 'or perhaps it was yours, Mabel – I told him it was for the lady in the brown hat,' and Auntie Mabel blushed and smiled and didn't seem to mind something conspicuous after all!

'Now *that*,' she exclaimed, when the last chord and the rapturous applause which followed it ('My Heart's Desire' seemed to have a very popular appeal) had died away, '*that*'s what I call *reely* beautiful, quite –'

She was interrupted by a sudden scream from Rosie. 'Jo, *Jo*!' she cried. 'Look at the clock! Look at the time ... our train ... oh, my goodness me – we'll never catch it ... and the last one as our tickets is good for ... quick, quick!'

How *could* they have forgotten? How *could* they! and with tickets only up to a certain time too!

'You'd best all stay here,' said Uncle Charlie to his

wife and the Perkins, 'while I see 'em to the station – I'll be
back in less than an hour. Keep calm now and we'll do it!'
he cried to the distracted Ruggles, and catching up their
bags and bundles, shouting good-byes and thank-yous,
they all scrambled after him into the lift, out into the street,
and (after an agonizing wait) on to a very crowded bus.

'We'll do it!' said Uncle Charlie at intervals, but he
had doubts. 'Have your tickets ready,' he said to his
brother, 'and we can run for it at the end – I'll take two
of the kids.' And run for it they did – Uncle Charlie with
Peg under one arm and Jo under the other, Rosie with
William (bleating), Lily Rose, Kate, and the twins panting in between, while Mr Ruggles, snowed under with
coats and bags – looking, as Uncle Charlie found time to
remark, like a stall from a jumble sale got loose – brought
up the rear.

'Too late!' said the ticket collector, and rudely slammed the platform gate in their faces; and there, just
beginning to move out of the station was their train!

William, expressing the feelings of the whole party, set
up a loud wail! . . .

'Where are you for?' asked a more polite official who
was standing near. 'Otwell – you're all right – we're
running another train . . . yes, your ticket'll do . . . platform fifteen . . . going in five minutes . . .'

The Ruggles had hardly enough breath left to reach
platform fifteen and every carriage in the train seemed full.
On and on they staggered, right down the long platform.

'Here you are – only two in here!' cried Uncle Charlie
at last, flinging open the door of the last carriage but one.
'In you get!' he cried, heaving the children in, one after
another. 'In you get, Rosie!'

Rosie, with William in her arms, flopped breathless
into a corner. A second later she was on her feet again,

And run for it they did

for there, facing her, a banana in her hand, her mouth, originally opened to take a bite, but now gaping wide with astonishment, was *Mrs Nosey Parker*, while in the further corner, his eyes fairly popping over the top of his newspaper, sat her husband! And it was not, Rosie quickly observed, a corridor train!

Meanwhile, Mr Ruggles, after one glance, was leaning out of the window murmuring something to his brother.

Putting William on the seat, Rosie pushed in beside him. 'Good-bye, Charlie dear!' she cried, holding out her hand. But Uncle Charlie was busy with his mouth organ.

Putting it to his lips, and gathering the little breath left in him, he started to play, and as the train began to move, Rosie caught the faint notes of an old song.

'What is it – what's he trying to play?' asked Mr Ruggles, as Uncle Charlie, running to keep up with the moving train, still valiantly attempted to wheeze out a tune. The train gathered speed, Uncle Charlie stopped running; Mrs Ruggles leant out for a last wave, then turning to her husband, she answered, '*The End of a Perfect Day*, dearie,' and kissed him on the nose!

Also by Eve Garnett

FURTHER ADVENTURES OF THE FAMILY FROM ONE END STREET

In this new book about the Ruggles Family, Mr and Mrs Ruggles are as short of money as ever. When the story begins three of the children have got measles, but this turns out to be a Blessing in Disguise for as a result Kate, Peg and Jo are sent on a convalescent holiday to a dream house in the country called the Dew Drop Inn, where they are looked after by Mrs Wildgoose, who must be the kindest landlady ever invented.

But as well as the excitements of the train journey and the joy of discovering the habits of the countryside, the family have other adventures – like the time Lily Rose is a bridesmaid, or when Mr Ruggles gets sent the wrong pig, or when Baby Ruggles sees a pussy-cat at the kitchen window and it turns out to be an escaped tiger. This story is every bit as good as the book you have just finished.